Shadow Mountain
LEONA KARR

MILLS & BOON®
Pure reading pleasure™

All the characters in this book have no existence outside
the imagination of the author, and have no relation
whatsoever to anyone bearing the same name or names.
They are not even distantly inspired by any individual
known or unknown to the author, and all the incidents
are pure invention.

All Rights Reserved including the right of reproduction
in whole or in part in any form. This edition is published
by arrangement with Harlequin Enterprises II BV/S.à.r.l.
The text of this publication or any part thereof may
not be reproduced or transmitted in any form or
by any means, electronic or mechanical, including
photocopying, recording, storage in an information
retrieval system, or otherwise, without the written
permission of the publisher.

® and TM are trademarks owned and used by the
trademark owner and/or its licensee. Trademarks marked
with ® are registered with the United Kingdom Patent
Office and/or the Office for Harmonisation in the
Internal Market and in other countries.

First published in Great Britain 2008
Large Print edition 2008
Harlequin Mills & Boon Limited,
Eton House, 18-24 Paradise Road,
Richmond, Surrey TW9 1SR

© Leona Karr 2007

ISBN: 978 0 263 20136 9

Set in Times Roman 17 on 21 pt.
34-0808-55243

Printed and bound in Great Britain
by Antony Rowe Ltd, Chippenham, Wiltshire

LEONA KARR

loves to read and write, and her favourite books are romantic suspense. Every book she writes is an exciting discovery as she finds the right combination of romance and intrigue. The majority of her novels are set in her home state, Colorado. When she's not reading and writing, she thoroughly enjoys spoiling her eight beautiful granddaughters.

To my husband, Michael,
whose love and laughter
inspire and enrich my life.

Chapter One

The clock in the hall had already struck midnight when Caroline Fairchild pushed back from her home computer. Muttering an unladylike expletive, she rubbed the tense muscles in her neck. The discouraging financial printout told her what she already knew. Her newly launched decorating business in Denver was in the red. If she didn't get at least one lucrative contract this fall, she'd lose the investment of her late husband's life insurance and probably the house, too.

It wasn't just her future that was at stake. There was Danny, her six-year-old son. Growing up without his father was hard enough. She wanted him to have a full and happy life. Being a single parent presented more challenges than she had ever imagined.

Wearily, she turned out the lights on the lower floor and went upstairs to Danny's bedroom.

"I'll figure something out," she whispered as she bent over the child's bed and brushed back his light-brown hair from his forehead. He was a beautiful child and her heart swelled with the miracle that he was hers. Since she had no other family, she'd wanted to be a mother more than anything in the world. Now that she had lost her husband, having this darling little boy to raise made every day a special blessing.

Quietly, she crossed the hall to her bedroom and left the door open in case Danny called to her. Even though her husband, Thomas, had been dead two years, being alone at night was still the hardest part of being a widow. She'd given up wearing the sexy nightgowns and settled for old-fashioned flannel pajamas. Sometimes when she looked in the mirror, she wondered where her youth had gone. Even though she'd kept herself physically fit and her hair was still a rich dark brown and her blue eyes were 20/20, she thought she looked older than her thirty-two years.

She lay awake for a long time, her thoughts heavy with unanswered questions and decisions to be made. The tiny bedside clock had passed two o'clock before her tense body began to relax. She was finally on the edge of sleep when suddenly her nostrils quivered with the stench of burning wood. She sat up and clasped a hand over her nose and mouth.

Smoke!

She leaped from the bed and bounded into the hall. Clouds of black smoke rolled up the stairway. Somewhere on the floor below was a terrifying brightness and the sound of crackling flames.

"Danny!" Shouting, she ran into his room and grabbed him up from the bed. Half-asleep, he started to fight her. "No, honey no, the house is on fire! We have to get out."

He was a load to carry as she fled back into the hall, holding him tightly against her chest. They had to get out of the house. Frightened, Danny began to cough and struggle in her arms.

The only exits from the house were on the ground floor. As she froze at the top of the stairs, she could see tongues of red flames already licking at the stairs and banister. In moments the entire staircase would be in flames. Black smoke swirled around them.

"I can't see," Danny wailed.

As she wavered at the top of the stairs, the heat rose up to meet her, instantly parching her mouth and throat with a burning dryness. Her eyes were watering and the biting smell of scorched wood and cloth seared her nostrils.

A dancing brightness at the bottom of the

stairway warned her that the entire first floor might already be a flaming furnace. Danny was coughing and crying as she plunged down the stairs through the swirling, thick haze.

Panic drove her through an encroaching ribbon of fire spreading along the bottom step. She leaped over it, almost losing her balance as she fled down the smoke-filled hall.

Fiery flames were devouring the dining-room curtains and spreading along the carpet runner leading to the front room. Danny bolted out of her arms with the panicked strength of a terrified six-year-old. He disappeared in the direction of the front foyer just as a thunderous crash vibrated through the depths of the house.

"Danny!" she screeched with parched lips and a burning throat as she ran after him. He was already at the locked front door, pounding on it and whimpering when she reached him. Her eyes were watering so badly, she couldn't see the dead bolt. As her hands played blindly on the door seeking it, her fingers touched a hinge. She was on the wrong side of the door!

Danny had his face buried against her night-gown when she finally found the lock. Frantically, she turned it with one hand and jerked open the door with the other.

They bounded outside.

Coughing and gasping, they stumbled across the porch and down the front steps. The sound of falling timbers and radiating heat from leaping flames followed them across the yard.

Grabbing Danny's hand, she croaked, "Run."

At two o'clock in the morning all was quiet in the modest neighborhood in North Denver. The street was empty of people and cars. Only a few porch lights were on as they bolted across the cul-de-sac to the house of Betty and Jim McClure, her closest neighbors and long-time friends.

They stumbled up the steps and Caroline's frantic ringing of the doorbell and pounding brought Jim, disheveled and sleepy-eyed, to the door.

His eyes widened when he saw them. "Caroline! What on earth? What's happened?"

"Call 9-1-1! Fire. My house!"

When Jim looked across the street and saw the flames leaping out of the windows and roof, he spun on his bare feet and ran for the phone.

"What is it?" Betty called from the top of the stairs and hurried down.

Caroline tried to answer but a spasm of coughing choked her words.

"Our house is on fire," Danny whimpered.

ALL NIGHT crews from two fire trucks fought to control the flames. Caroline knew she never would forget the sound of the wailing sirens and the sight of firemen mobilizing to fight a dangerous enemy.

By sunup, their victory was small.

A stench of smoke, ashes and foul water

floated through the whole neighborhood. The entire house had been gutted. The back was leveled. Most of the roof on the remainder had collapsed and water damage was everywhere.

As Caroline stared at the devastation, her lips quivered with disbelief. She and Thomas had bought the house when they were first married.

It had been the only real home she'd ever had. Her parents had been dryland farmers in eastern Colorado, moving from one acreage to another when times were bad—and they always were. Caroline was an only child and had been weighed down with responsibility and never-ending poverty as she grew up. Her parents had died within a year of each other when she was a senior in high school. She'd always been a hard worker and good student and her perfect 4.0 high-school record earned her a full scholarship to Colorado University.

She'd been working in the cafeteria when she met Thomas Fairchild, an older medical student doing his internship. Thomas always told her she was the prettiest girl with summer-blue eyes and soft brown hair that he'd ever seen. Their marriage had been a happy one, especially after Danny had become a part of their lives.

Now, she bit her lip to fight the ache in her heart as she walked across the street and stared at the shambles of their home. Most of the firemen had left, but the fire chief had remained. His expression was sympathetic as he walked over to her.

"I'm afraid there's not much left."

"But surely, I haven't lost everything?" she asked, biting her lip to control her emotions.

He avoided a direct answer. "Do you have any idea what started the blaze?"

She shook her head. "I can't imagine how it happened."

"Did you have any combustible material stored at the back of the house or in the kitchen?" he prodded.

"No. And nothing left on the stove. I always clean up after dinner and work a few hours in my office."

His eyes traveled over what was left of the house. "I'm afraid the damage is extensive."

"I'll need to go through and see what I can salvage," she said in a strained voice.

"Maybe tomorrow," he hedged. "You'll have to have one of the firemen go with you." He cleared his throat. "The cause of the fire is under investigation. We don't want any potential evidence destroyed. Arson is always a possibility."

The way his eyes narrowed suggested he was considering the idea that she'd set it herself.

She stiffened. "How long will the investigation take?"

"Hard to tell."

Caroline knew that meant the insurance company was absolved of any responsibility to write out a check for who knew how long.

THREE DAYS passed before she was finally allowed inside the house. In the company of a young fireman, she went through the painful process of salvaging what she could.

She was relieved that her important personal papers and a few old photos of her late parents were in a metal box that had survived the heat. Her office was destroyed.

Nothing in the upstairs rooms was salvageable. What hadn't burned was ruined by smoke and water. When all was said and done, she accepted the stark reality that all was gone.

She was grateful for the generosity of friends and strangers and, luckily, she had just taken some fall and winter clothes to the cleaners to get ready for the October weather. She had no choice but to use funds from her less-than-impressive bank account to buy necessities for her and Danny.

"What are you going to do, Caroline?" Betty

asked as Caroline sat dejectedly in the kitchen, staring at a cup of tea. "I mean about your business? I know you've always worked out of your home but you're welcome to put in a desk at our furniture store."

Jim and Betty owned the McClure Furniture Outlet and it was through their referral of some of their customers that Caroline had secured several redecorating contracts.

"Maybe that way you'll pick up some decorating jobs from more of our customers," Betty encouraged. "And you and Danny can stay with us until things get settled."

"That's kind of you. I just don't know."

After the shock had worn off and reality set in, Caroline gratefully accepted both offers.

Danny had turned six the first week in October—after school had started, so he was in kindergarten.

Betty loaned Caroline a laptop and she set up her "office" in a corner of their store.

Using the telephone, she prospected for viable clients and created a simple advertising brochure to hand out.

She had just hung up the telephone, batting zero for the morning, when Betty and an attractive woman approached her desk.

"Caroline, I want you to meet Stella Wainwright. She's from Texas and her brother-in-law has a mountain lodge in Colorado that he's decided to redecorate."

"Pleased to meet you." Caroline rose to her feet and held out her hand. "Caroline Fairchild."

The woman was fashionably dressed in gabardine slacks, a pink knit shell and a leather jacket. Her blondish hair was cut short around a tanned face and alert hazel eyes matched her steady expression. Caroline guessed her to be close to forty despite her youthful appearance.

"She tells me she's having trouble hiring a decorator willing to go and work in such an isolated place," Betty explained quickly. "I told her I didn't know whether you'd be interested—with your other commitments and all," she added with a straight face.

"The project sounds interesting," Caroline responded, smiling and playing the role of a successful, busy decorator.

With obvious satisfaction, Betty made her retreat, leaving the two women to talk.

"Please sit down." Caroline motioned to a nearby chair and turned her desk chair in that direction. "Where is the lodge located?"

"At the foot of the San Juan Mountains on the western slope of Colorado," she answered, crossing her legs in a relaxed fashion.

"Near Durango?"

"North of there. Closer to Telluride."

"I see." Caroline had never been in that part of the state but she had a general idea of the area.

"His property is extensive and includes its own lake and encompasses hundreds of acres of mountain forest," Stella Wainwright continued. "The lodge is quite isolated and private."

Caroline mentally groaned. The nearby Rocky Mountains were great for an occasional recreational pastime, but working in a rugged, isolated area of the state with a six-year-old boy wasn't high on Caroline's preference list.

"I'm not sure," Caroline began.

"I know what you're thinking." The other woman gave a light laugh. "It's not that bad, trust me. The Wainwright family built Shadow Mountain Lodge as a welcome retreat for family and friends from hot, muggy Texas summer heat. My late husband, Delvin, loved it. He was Wes's younger brother and was killed in a private plane crash en route to the lodge."

"Oh, I'm sorry," Caroline said sincerely; she knew what it was like to lose a husband.

"My teenage son, Shane, and I still spend a good deal of time at the lodge. It's isolated and set on the slopes of Shadow Mountain. The surroundings are quite beautiful."

"I'm sure they are," Caroline replied evenly. Without even seeing the place, she was intimidated by the challenges such a job would present. The demands of acquiring materials and dependable labor to carry out a job there could be a living nightmare.

Before Caroline could put her refusal in polite terms, Stella Wainwright surprised her by reaching out and touching her hand. "I can assure you that Wesley Wainwright, heir to the family's oil empire, would financially make it worth your time and effort." In the next breath, she mentioned a figure that was ten times what Caroline had expected.

"For that amount of money, you could hire the very best—"

"I've tried," Stella replied shortly. "All the interior decorators I have on my list have refused for one reason or another. Maybe it's because I have very definite ideas about what I want done. Of course, sometimes those ideas change when I don't quite like the way they work out."

Uh-oh, enough said! Now Caroline understood! Stella Wainwright was looking for someone who would put up with her constantly changing her mind about what she wanted. A decorator's nightmare!

As if to verify Caroline's thoughts, Stella gave Caroline a measuring look and asked, "Do you think we could work together?"

The innocent question was loaded. Caroline knew it. If she accepted this job it would probably turn out to be pure hell. She'd bet there would be plenty of headaches with little satisfaction. Maybe even the loss of her own integrity included.

She wanted to say, "No thanks. I'll pass." But she didn't. There were too many things at stake, like securing an immediate income and having a place for her and Danny to stay without imposing on anyone. Her options were painfully limited. When it came down to it, she really didn't have a choice.

She straightened her shoulders and replied in a calm and rational tone, "Yes, I think we could work together nicely, Mrs. Wainwright."

"Call me Stella," the woman invited with a smile that sealed the matter. "How soon do you think you could begin?"

WESLEY WAINWRIGHT had just come back to the lodge from a hike on Shadow Mountain when the phone rang. He was breathing a little heavily when he answered it. The climb was always a strenuous one, but his six-foot body had handled the muscular demands with ease and he felt as strong now in his thirties as he had in college. He loved being out in the mountain air, away from closed-in offices, board meetings and the ever-present demands of his financial responsibilities.

He sighed as he picked up the receiver. If it was his secretary in Houston, he was going to hang up.

"Hi, it's Stella."

His sister-in-law had been gone nearly a week and he'd rather enjoyed not having her around. Sometimes Stella's presence got a little tedious. He wasn't all that happy when she'd showed up at the lodge during his planned vacation away from work and family. Frankly, he'd been relieved when she'd left to spend time in Denver. She was one of those women who liked to manage everything and everybody—including him.

"What's happening?" he asked in a guarded tone. Stella's voice was laced with excitement.

"It wasn't easy but I did it. I found one."

"One what?"

"An interior decorator," she answered impatiently. "I found one who will come to the lodge.

Last spring we talked about doing some redecorating at the lodge. Don't you remember?"

Wes's hand tightened on the receiver. "I thought that was in the future." *Way in the future,* he added silently. "I didn't know you were intending to carry out the idea so soon."

"I just haven't been able to find a decorator who would spend several months isolated in the mountains—until today."

"When is all of this going to start happening?" His sister-in-law was constantly testing his patience. If she hadn't been his late brother's widow, he wouldn't have put up with her being such a controlling force in his life.

"Since it's early October, everything will be just perfect for the Christmas holidays. I've arranged for the decorator to start next week. Her name is Caroline Fairchild and she'll be bringing her little boy with her." She paused. "I'm thinking of putting them in rooms on the second floor. She'll need another room close by to work in. Since your suite is at the far end of the corridor you won't be bothered. What do you think?"

He controlled an impulse to tell her exactly what he thought. "Yes, fine."

"Good. They'll arrive next week."

Wesley hung up the phone, muttering, "Well, so much for peace and quiet."

Having Stella show up had been bad enough but now she was arranging for some decorator and her kid to move in for God knew how long. Stella had been twenty-four years old when she'd married his nineteen-year-old brother, Delvin. Noticeably pregnant at the time, Stella eventually gave birth to a baby boy they named Shane. To her credit, since Delvin's death almost six years ago, Stella had been a conscientious single mother to her son.

Wes had tried to fill in the empty spot that his brother's death had left in the boy's life. Now seventeen, Shane loved spending time in

Colorado. The young man had made it clear he'd rather forget about college and just enjoy life on the ski slopes and hiking trails. His mother disagreed, but Wes thought it might be a good idea for Shane to take a year off, to discover a few things about himself.

Wes always tried his best to accommodate Stella's ideas and plans when they were at the lodge but this latest decorating craze of hers was the limit.

He could imagine the frenzy the lodge would be in when the redecorating got into full swing. Well, he wasn't going to stick around to see it. He'd be long gone. There were plenty of spots in Colorado where a man could find peace and quiet.

He reached for some brochures and settled back to make plans for his escape.

Chapter Two

The Wainwright property on the southern edge of the Colorado San Juan Mountains was a seven-hour drive from Denver. A narrow road twisted through rugged shadowy slopes that reminded Caroline of pictures she'd seen of Germany's brooding Black Forest.

"Are we there yet?" Danny asked in a bored voice.

"Almost." She sent him a reassuring smile that faked the confidence she didn't feel.

"I'm tired."

"Me, too." She'd turned off the main highway hours ago and had no idea how close she was to the Wainwright lodge. Only vaulting wooded cliffs rose on each side, making a tunnel-like passage for the twisting mountain road. Signs of habitation were scarce and the pencil map Stella had drawn was of little help. She'd made an *X* to show where the lodge stood at one end of a small, private lake—but where was the lake?

Caroline's hands were tense on the steering wheel as she maneuvered a series of hairpin curves. Then, suddenly, without warning, there was a break in the view ahead and a startling vista opened up before her eyes. Nestled in the circle of the encroaching mountains was a meadow, a small lake and an access road posted with a wooden sign, Shadow Mountain Lodge.

"We're here," she said with a sigh of relief.

Danny peered over the front seat as best he could, straining against his seatbelt. "Where? I don't see nothing."

"Anything," she automatically corrected him.

"See that building across the lake? That's where we're going."

He stuck out his lower lip the way he did when things weren't going his way. When they got closer, he said, "I hate it. It's ugly."

Caroline wasn't about to argue. Built of austere, dark wood, the mountain lodge was set in the depths of towering trees that hugged its square, unrelieved lines. A late-afternoon sun failed to lighten the blankness of recessed dormer windows crouched under a sharply slanted roof.

She remembered Stella had told her that her brother-in-law was a widower and had a six-year-old daughter named Cassie. Caroline hoped that Danny and the little girl got along. Her son was easygoing most of the time but when Danny set his mind against some thing or someone, a team of horses couldn't budge him.

She followed the road that bordered the lake and then rose sharply to the lodge set against the steep backdrop of a mountain. She continued past the lodge and parked in an open area which looked as if it might lead to some other smaller buildings like stables and bunkhouses set back in the trees.

Once released from his seat, Danny bounded out of the car like a young animal freed from a cage.

"Stay close," she ordered as she took out an overnight bag and decided to leave the rest of the luggage until later. The place looked deserted, but she could hear the neighing of a horse and spied a corral set back in the trees.

With Danny at her side, they walked around to the front of the lodge and climbed a flight of wooden stairs to a heavy, planked front door. A brass lion's head with its mouth open made a loud clanging sound as she dropped the knocker several times.

As they waited, she rested her hand reassuringly on Danny's shoulder but already the enveloping isolation was getting to her. Her mouth went dry.

What on earth am I doing here?

The massive door suddenly opened and Stella stood there, smiling at them. "Oh, good, I was hoping you'd get here before dark. Sometimes these mountain roads can be a little tricky at night."

Caroline silently added, *And in daylight.* It was some kind of miracle she'd found the place at all.

"Please come in. I'll send Shane to bring in the rest of your luggage."

They followed her inside and the interior of the lodge seemed just as dark and intimidating as the exterior. Beyond a shadowy vestibule, they entered a large room with a high ceiling and a monstrous chandelier made of elk horns suspended from a high rafter. Several tall windows allowed muted sunlight to slightly relieve the shadows of high ceilings and dark-panelled walls. A massive stone fireplace dominated the far wall and a variety of furniture, mostly leather and dark walnut, was scattered about. An area rug of faded green covered a small section of a wide-planked floor. Some framed black-and-white photographs hung on the wall. They were group pictures as far as Caroline could tell. She wondered if this was one of the rooms Stella wanted redecorated. If so, simply introducing some color would be a step in the right direction.

"I'll show you to your rooms first," Stella said motioning toward a massive staircase mounting a far wall. "You'll probably want to freshen up before meeting Wes. He was set to leave yesterday when one of his good friends, Dexter Tate, showed up unexpectedly. They're out target-shooting but should be back anytime. Wes's daughter, Cassie, is upstairs with her nanny, Felicia." She glanced at her watch. "I'd better see that some refreshment is ready."

As they mounted the steps to the second floor and walked a short distance down the hall, Stella said in a practiced hostess manner, "I hope you'll be comfortable here. There's a small sitting room, a bedroom with twin beds and a connecting bath. I've set up a workroom just down the hall. If there's anything I've missed, just let me know."

She opened the door and motioned them inside. They had just walked into the sitting room when Danny suddenly cowered beside her, hugging her leg.

"What is it?" She followed his frightened gaze to the walls of the room. Her breath caught. "Good heavens!"

Mounted on the walls were heads of wild animals—a fierce black bear, a threatening mountain lion and a snarling wildcat. She could tell from the raw fear in Danny's expression that he thought they were alive and about to jump down on him.

"It's all right, honey," Caroline said quickly. "They won't hurt you."

"They're dead?"

"Yes. Somebody killed them."

"Why?" he demanded with childish bluntness.

"They're like trophies," Stella answered quickly before Caroline could. "Big men shoot them and then hang them on the walls to show how brave they are. I'm afraid you'll find them all over the lodge." Then she brightened. "But your mother and I are going to make some nice changes."

Caroline didn't say anything, but she wondered how easy that was going to be. Changing anything that had become a male tradition might be an uphill battle. If she were a gambler, she'd bet the mounted animals stayed despite Stella's best efforts.

Fortunately the small bedroom was spared any hunting decor. Several scenic pictures hung on the walls. One window had simple green draperies hanging from a brass rod. Caroline was delighted with the hand-crafted aspen bedroom furniture. She immediately visualized how a little color and fresh wallpaper would add a pleasant warmth to the room.

"If there's anything you need, just let me know," Stella said, preparing to leave them. "Please come downstairs when you're ready. There's a small social room just past the main stairs and down the hall. I know Wes will be pleased to meet you both. He has a little girl about your age, Danny. Her name is Cassie. I know you'll have fun playing with her while your mother and I are busy."

Danny's scowl plainly showed his reaction to the idea. Girls weren't his thing.

Caroline silently sighed. A belligerent little six-year-old was all she needed to make this whole experience a living nightmare. Her son's mood certainly didn't improve when she insisted on a hands-and-face washing, a quick change of clothes and a brushing of his tousled brown hair. He flopped down on one of the beds while she freshened up.

Stella had warned her they'd need warm clothes as well as walking shoes and boots. Caroline had followed her suggestions and found some bargains for her and Danny that she could afford.

She wanted to make a good first impression. After exchanging her jeans for a pair of tan slacks and her plain pullover for a variegated knit sweater in the red and orange colors of fall leaves, a quick glance in the mirror warned her she didn't look very professional. Somehow her two tailored outfits didn't seem right either. Besides, they were packed in the luggage she'd left in the car. She brushed her lips lightly with pink gloss, gave her short, wavy hair a quick combing and straightened her shoulders.

"I guess I'm ready," she said as she came out of the bathroom. When she saw that Danny had fallen asleep, she groaned. Now what? She couldn't leave him here asleep. If he woke up and was alone with all those animal heads, he'd freak out! But he'd be grumpy if he didn't have a nap.

Stella would probably be waiting impatiently, but she didn't have a choice. Caroline knew she'd have to wait at least a half hour before waking him.

As she looked at his sweet face, so angelic in sleep, her chest was suddenly tight with emotion. He was so precious. Her whole life now. He'd been only two years old when she was left to raise him alone. Even though Thomas's medical career had dominated his time and energies, his unexpected heart attack and death had left her without any emotional support. There were no grandparents or close relatives to provide an extended family for either of them.

She turned away from the bed and walked

over to the window to look out. Her view was of the wooded slopes behind the lodge. Already the sun had slipped behind craggy mountain peaks and she would have missed seeing the two horsemen moving through the trees if their movement had not caught her eye. Before she could get a good look at them, they disappeared beyond her view.

Wes Wainwright, no doubt, and the guest Stella mentioned who had gone target-shooting with him. She wondered what targets they'd chosen for their sport and doubted that she could even be polite to her Texas host after seeing the mounted heads.

She'd always had trouble controlling her temper when she encountered selfish, self-centered men. Bragging rich Texans who seemed to throw their weight around had never been very high on her list.

When she finally woke Danny, he was less than cooperative.

"When can we go home?" he said with a scowl as she brushed his hair once again.

"Not today," she said with false cheerfulness. She couldn't tell him when it would be because she really didn't know the answer. Everything depended upon Stella and her redecorating plans. If they were superficial and limited, the job would only require a few weeks. If the entire lodge was to undergo a coordinated redecoration, several months might be involved.

"I bet you're hungry." Caroline said brightly. "Let's go downstairs and have a nice dinner."

She was glad a bedroom door led into the hall so they didn't have to go through the sitting room with the overpowering animal heads. Danny needed time to adjust to this strange environment.

And so do I!

Their feet made a muffled sound on the bare steps as they descended the staircase to the main room. Someone had turned on a few scattered lights that played over the furniture, gloomy walls and stone fireplace. The bulbs on the ugly antler chandelier remained dark as it hung like a menacing threat overhead.

Following Stella's instructions, Caroline turned down a dimly lit hall and, with Danny hugging her side, passed a series of doors opening into various sized rooms. She couldn't tell what they were used for because they were all dark.

Caroline was beginning to wonder if she'd missed the right way when she heard the sound of voices and saw light spilling through double doors opening into the hall.

She tried for a composed smile when they entered the social room, as Stella had called it. Even though the decor was much the same as the main room's—paneled walls and brown leather furniture—the warmth and lighting in the room was a sharp contrast to

the rest of the lodge. The room gave off a surprising cheerfulness.

She held Danny's tense little hand firmly as
he started to pull back. She saw then he was
staring at a black bear skin with an snarling,
open mouth stretched out above the fireplace.

Stella immediately stood up from a chair
next to a coffee table. "There you are. I was
about to send someone after you. I want you
to meet Wes."

Caroline could tell she was nervous. *Maybe
as nervous as I am.* "I'm sorry, Danny took a
little nap and delayed us."

Two men stood in front of a blazing fireplace
with drinks in their hands. *Which one is the
Texas tycoon?* Was it the overweight, round-
faced fellow wearing leather trousers and a
fringed jacket? The one doing all the talking
and gesturing with his free hand?

The other man was taller, well-proportioned,
wearing jeans and a denim shirt open at the

collar and rolled up at the cuffs. A shock of brown hair with a glint of red hung low on his forehead and framed a strong, masculine face.

A slight frown creased his forehead as Stella brought Caroline across the room and introduced her. "Wes, this is Caroline Fairchild and her son, Danny. She's the decorator," she added as a reminder.

"Oh, yes. Pleased to meet you," he replied politely and Caroline sensed a decided lack of enthusiasm in his manner.

"Did you kill that?" Danny demanded, thrusting a pointing finger up at the mounted bear skin.

"Nope. My grandpa killed that one."

"Why?"

"Well, that old bear was looking around for something to eat. You can see his sharp teeth. Grandpa didn't want him to have his dog, Shep, for dinner. My little girl says he looks mean. What do you think?"

"I don't like him," Danny answered flatly.

"Smart boy." He nodded approvingly. "How old are you, Danny?"

"Six."

"Really? What do you know? I have a little girl the same age." He turned to Caroline. "They're a handful, aren't they?" She could tell he was forcing himself to be congenial so she smiled and nodded.

Obviously, he wasn't all that pleased about having an interior decorator under foot. Something warned her that she'd better tread softly and keep her distance. If he was going to pay her the exorbitant amount Stella had promised, she couldn't afford to antagonize him. She remembered Stella had said he had intended to be gone before she arrived. Caroline suspected that under those good looks there was probably plenty of barbed wire.

Despite Wes's lack of enthusiasm, Stella seemed to be determined to proceed full speed ahead with the project. "We'll be looking over the lodge and deciding where to begin—"

"Just leave my suite and the gun room alone." His tone brooked no argument. The lines and planes in his face suggested a firm control of his thoughts and feelings. Even when he smiled his eyes held a certain glint, as if his mind were functioning on many levels. He was worth millions and his casual attire didn't fool Caroline a bit. She suspected only a fool would judge him by outward appearances.

The robust man still standing by the fireplace chuckled as he took another drink from his glass. He must be the old friend Stella said had arrived unexpectedly. As the man's assessing eyes traveled over her, Caroline mentally stiffened against his open appraisal. They hadn't even met yet and she didn't like him.

At that moment, a little girl bounded into the room, blond pigtails flapping. She was wearing jeans and a plaid shirt. A red cowboy hat hung by a string down her back. When she saw Danny, she stopped short.

"Who's that?" she demanded, scowling.

Danny's little mouth tightened as he scowled back.

"This is Danny Fairchild, Cassie," Stella answered quickly in a warning tone. "He's going to be a guest at the lodge and you'll want to make him feel welcome."

"What if I don't like him?"

Oh, no, thought Caroline. *This could turn out to be a real nightmare.*

"What's not to like, honey?" her father asked as he motioned Cassie over to his side. "You've been complaining about not having anyone to go horseback-riding with you. How about it, son? Would you like to take a ride on one of Cassie's Shetland ponies?"

As Danny's scowl instantly faded, Caroline stiffened with sudden irritation. How dare this man make such an offer without knowing whether her son would be safe riding a horse—pony or otherwise.

Danny's eyes were already sparkling with anticipation as he looked up at her. "Mom…?"

"We'll see."

"Spoken like a true mother," quipped the man in leather trousers before Wes had a chance to say anything. As he stepped forward, he held out a pudgy hand. "Dexter Tate. Wes didn't warn me that we were going to have feminine company or I would have shaved for the occasion." He rubbed a growth of dark whiskers on his full cheeks and chin.

"Dexter thinks of himself as a ladies' man and we try to humor him," Wes said with a chuckle. Dexter took a playful swipe at him and they both laughed like good friends who enjoyed ribbing each other.

Cassie had moved closer to Danny. "You want to go see my ponies?"

"Not now, Cassie," her father said before Danny could respond. "It's almost time for dinner." He turned to Caroline. "I imagine it's been a long day. Traveling is never easy."

"Not unless you have a jet plane, helicopter and a slick foreign car," Dexter quipped and added with pointed emphasis, "Not that Wes ever travels alone."

"Cut it out, you two," Stella said quickly, obviously wanting to change the conversation.

A tall, lanky youth with a tanned narrow face and longish unkempt dark hair appeared in the doorway. He was wearing cowboy boots, a Western shirt and low-slung jeans held in place by a leather belt with a huge silver and turquoise buckle.

"Come in, Shane," Stella said with a wave of her hand.

"Cook says grub's on. Come and get it," he said as he ambled in with his hands in his pockets.

"Shane, that's no way to announce dinner. I

want you to meet Mrs. Fairchild. This is my seventeen-year-old son, Shane."

"Nice to meet you," Caroline quickly responded. "This is my son, Danny."

Shane gave a quick bob of his head at the introductions and as if to ward off a lecture from his mother, he told Caroline, "I took your suitcases up to your rooms."

She quickly thanked him and was rewarded with a fleeting smile that didn't quite meet his light-brown eyes.

"Shane's a big help around here," Wesley said as he put his arm around the adolescent's shoulders.

Caroline could tell that Shane was pleased with the attention. He ducked his head and shuffled his feet as if a little embarrassed by his uncle's attention.

"Shane's only going to spend a year here in Colorado before going to college," his mother said quickly as if there might have been some heated discussion about it. "His late father would have wanted him to fill his shoes, being responsible and taking care of family business. That means some brain work and study."

Caroline could tell from Shane's expression that he'd heard this lecture before. His eyes darkened. The young man's suddenly stiff posture hinted at an explosive emotion close to the surface.

Wes murmured, "Easy does it."

There was something threatening and unsettling about Shane Wainwright. Caroline decided then and there to keep Danny as far away from him as she could.

Chapter Three

Caroline was relieved that dinner was a casual affair served in a square room that resembled a café more than a formal dining area. The walls were knotty pine and undressed windows with open shutters overlooked a rocky slope and the lake below. Small maple tables and chairs were scattered around the room with no sign of the traditional long table. She suspected the lodge's main dining room was closed off when so few people were in residence.

Stella had told Caroline that usually only relatives and close friends made use of the lodge, but Wes invited business associates and acquaintances to be guests a few times during the year.

Wes and Dexter had stayed behind to finish their drinks and the only occupant in the room when Caroline, Stella and the children entered was a woman with graying dark hair and strong Spanish features sitting at one of the tables. Her dress was a bright, exotic print with a matching fringed shawl and a stream of different colored beads hung around her neck. Large silver hoops dangled from her ears.

"Nanny, here's another kid," Cassie exclaimed as she bounded over to her. Pointing a finger at Danny, she added with a frown, "I don't like him much. Does he get to play with all my things?"

The woman slowly set down her cup and rose to her feet. She was tall with a rather regal posture. Caroline guessed her to be in her fifties.

"No, sit down, Felicia," Stella ordered, but the woman remained standing as Stella drew Caroline forward. "I spoke to you about Mrs. Fairchild and her son being with us for a few weeks. Well, this is Danny. He's the same age as Cassie."

Felicia's dark eyes narrowed and she seemed to stiffen as she looked at Danny. Caroline wondered if she had already decided that the boy's presence spelled trouble.

"I'm sure having someone for Cassie to play with will be a help," Stella told her.

Caroline spoke up rather defensively. "Danny's preschool teachers have found him easy to manage. He plays well with other children. If there's any problem, I'll want to know about it."

"Such beautiful brown eyes, round and clear," Felicia said, her expression softening as she looked at him.

Cassie shook her finger at Danny in a warning manner. "You have to do as she says."

Danny stuck his tongue out at the bossy little girl.

To Caroline's surprise Felicia laughed

deeply, her earrings jingling as she nodded. Apparently, Danny's rejection of Cassie's bossiness amused her. "He's a nice boy. You bring him to my rooms. We'll all play and learn together."

"Good. That's settled then," Stella said, just as Wes and Dexter came into the room.

"Mmm. Smells good," Dexter said. "I'm hungry as a bear. Grrrr," he said patting his stomach as he made a play move for Danny. He laughed when Danny backed up and gave him a wide-eyed stare.

"That's enough, Dex," Wes said and motioned Caroline and Danny toward a built-in buffet along one wall. "We don't stand on formality here. We serve ourselves except for drinks."

"Wait for me at a table, Danny," Caroline told him. "I'll bring you a plate."

The choices were unbelievable and Caroline decided there were enough steaming dishes set out to feed a harvest crew. She had a choice of chicken, roast beef or barbecue pork ribs. There were several vegetable casseroles and potatoes oozing with butter. A platter of fruit was about the only thing that didn't shriek calories.

Caroline selected a piece of chicken, modest servings of two kinds of vegetables and sliced oranges for both her and Danny. Wes, Dexter and Shane were in line behind her, filling their plates to the fullest.

Stella and Cassie took their plates to the table where Danny was sitting and as Caroline followed, she noticed that Felicia had left. She wondered if it was the nanny's habit not to eat with the family.

As the two men and Shane sat together at another table, a murmur of conversation and laughter filled the small room. Almost immediately, as if there'd been some kind of signal to the kitchen, a rather plump, redheaded woman in slacks and T-shirt came into the room to serve the drinks.

"Trudie Benson, our housekeeper," Stella told Caroline. "Her husband, Hank, is our wonderful cook and the two of them keep the place going. They're recruits from the Texas ranch. Been with the Wainwright family for years. Wes brought them to Colorado when he was first married."

"How long ago was that?"

"Before I was born," Cassie piped up. "Daddy told me. Him and Mommy were lonesome until I came along. When she went to heaven, he was glad he still had me."

"My daddy went to heaven, too," Danny said as if he wasn't going to be outdone. "And my mom's glad she has me."

Both Caroline and Stella choked back smiles. Competitive natures, both of them.

Caroline begged off staying downstairs after dinner. It had been a long day and both she and Danny were tired. To her surprise, Wes invited her to have an after-dinner drink before retiring, but she politely refused. She knew better than to fraternize with the boss.

After they were settled in their beds and Danny had said his prayers, she wearily closed her eyes and courted sleep. None came. After an hour of turning and tossing, she was still awake. The dynamics of her new situation and the people she'd met kept her mind whirling.

Wes Wainwright certainly had perfected an image of devoted father and unpretentious millionaire. But was it just a facade? What was he like, really? She doubted that he'd stay around long enough for her to find out. Even if he did, she was pretty sure he'd make his presence scarce while the redecorating was going on.

And what about Stella and her son, Shane? Stella must have been much older than the younger brother, Delvin, to marry and have a son of seventeen. She wondered what Wes's wife had been like and what had happened to her. Caroline tossed all of this around in her mind until she finally fell into a restless sleep.

The room was filled with morning light when she came awake with a jerk. Danny was bending over her, his breath warm on her face. "Are you awake?"

"Almost," she said and smiled as she cupped his face with her hands and kissed his forehead. "Are you?"

"Can we go home, now?"

"Not today."

"When can we?"

"I'm not sure," she answered honestly. Taking one day at a time was the only way she could cope at the moment. She wasn't at all sure how this decorating job was going to play out. Stella's temperament was certainly a question mark. Conceivably, the woman could throw her hands up at any time and fire Caroline without much cause.

Obviously, her brother-in-law, Wes, had no

emotional investment in the project. Caroline suspected he'd be glad enough to have the whole idea scrapped.

And then there was Cassie. If Danny got cross-wise with her in any serious way, her father would promptly show them the door to keep her happy. And Felicia wasn't exactly the kind of nanny Caroline would have chosen. She didn't seem the type who easily related to children.

WES WAS the only one in the room when they came down to breakfast. He watched as Caroline and Danny moved along the buffet. When she gave him a hesitant smile, he was glad he'd made the effort to come down early. He stood up and motioned for them to join him at his table.

He thought she looked trim and neat in light-blue slacks, matching jacket and simple white blouse. The first thing he'd noticed about her was her eyes. They were as blue and clear as a summer's sky. Her brunette, wavy hair was short, casual and carefree. He liked that. He couldn't stand women who were always fussing with their hair. His late wife, Pamela, had been the worst. She'd been a Texas beauty queen when he'd met and married her. Her appearance had always been uppermost in her mind. It got a little wearying at times.

As they sat down, Wes poured her coffee from a table carafe and offered Danny a carton of chocolate milk.

"I like chocolate best," Danny said with a happy grin.

"I thought you might," he said smiling as he poured it into a glass for him. He was a damn cute kid. Not as outgoing as Cassie, but he'd bet Danny was just as sure of himself in his own way. "Did you sleep well?" he asked Caroline as if the dark circles under her eyes weren't answer enough.

"So-so. I guess I had a few things on my mind."

As she sipped her coffee and looked at him over the rim of her cup, a feeling he hadn't experienced for a long time stirred within him. Her features were totally feminine and her full breasts and rounded hips invited the caressing touch of a man's hands. Her lips were moist and pink from the warmth of the hot coffee and he couldn't help but imagine what they would feel like pressed against his. As he felt desire begin to stir, he looked away quickly and gave his attention to his cinnamon toast.

"Lovely view," she said, looking out the window.

"This early in the morning the sun just brushes the tops of the trees," he told her. "The mountains look as if they've been painted against the sky. As far as I'm concerned, the Colorado Rockies have the kind of beauty that makes life worthwhile. I hope you can relax, Caroline, and enjoy yourself a little while you're here."

"Stella said you wouldn't be staying."

Wes couldn't tell from her tone whether it made the slightest difference to her one way or the other. He was used to women who welcomed his company and for some strange reason he wanted her to be one of them.

"I've changed my plans a bit—because of Dexter. I guess I'll have to keep him company for a few days at least."

The excuse was a lie. Dexter often spent time at the lodge or Wes's Texas ranch when Wes wasn't around. His old friend had been trying to make time with Stella for quite a while— without much luck. If Stella favored anyone it was Tim Henderson, the manager-caretaker of the property. Tim was a little older than Stella, quiet-spoken and didn't jump when she threw her weight around. Their relationship hadn't changed much through the years and Wes really didn't know if they had a private, intimate relationship going or not.

"I hope Dex and I won't be in your way,"

Wes added, blatantly fishing for an assurance his presence would be welcome.

"I'm not sure how extensive Stella's plans are," she replied evenly.

"You may have trouble putting a leash on Stella's wild ideas," he warned.

"That isn't my job. I've been hired to follow her wishes as best I can. My commitment is to please Stella and offer suggestions, but not implement my own ideas."

"Then heaven help us both," he said lightly. He was impressed with the firm way she set him straight. He liked that.

"More coffee?" he asked as he filled her cup.

Danny piped up. "Where's that girl?"

"You mean Cassie?"

Danny bobbed his head. "Yeah, her."

"She usually has breakfast and sometimes lunch with her nanny upstairs. They have a nice little kitchen apartment all their own. Maybe you'd like to join them sometime?"

Danny's expression clearly expressed his lack of enthusiasm for such a happening. "I don't like girls."

Wes chuckled at the child's display of disgust. Danny was all boy. Watching a son like that grow up would be a joy. Wes's heart tightened just a bit. He loved his daughter, but he couldn't help wishing he also had his own son to raise.

"Girls are a pest sometimes," he agreed solemnly. "It's too bad you're not interested though. Cassie has a playroom filled with all kinds of fun things. And then there're the ponies."

"I'm not sure that's a good idea," his mother said quickly. "Danny's never been around horses."

"Maybe this is a good time to give him that opportunity. One of my staff, Tim Henderson, is very good with youngsters. He rides with Cassie almost every day." Wes could tell she wasn't sold on the idea. "What about you? Have you done any horseback riding?"

Her laughter surprised him. "I've ridden bareback, saddled up my own mount and even mucked out a stable or two." She told him that her parents had been farm people.

"Well, I guess I'd better brush up on my own performance before asking you to go riding with me."

"We could all go," Danny popped up in a firm little voice.

Wes was beginning to like this kid more and more. "Good idea. How about this after-noon?"

"Oh, I don't know. Stella—" Caroline started to protest.

"Let's say four o'clock. She should be through with you by then."

"Please, Mama, please," Danny begged.

Wes could tell Danny's mother was hard put to deny his eager expression. "We ought to take advantage of the nice weather. October can be unpredictable, especially in the high country."

"All right, if Stella doesn't object."

"Good," Wes stood up and ruffled Danny's hair. "See you then, cowboy."

CAROLINE AND Danny were just finishing their breakfast when Trudie Benson came in from the kitchen. She wiped her hands on an apron large enough to cover her rounded middle and asked, "Everything all right?"

"Great," Caroline assured her. "Thank you."

"No need for thanks. Hank and I are happy just to see people enjoying the food."

"Where is everybody?"

"The hired help eat early and the rest eat late. You're kinda in the middle. Felicia and Cassie are having breakfast upstairs."

"Could you tell me where their rooms are? I need to check with the nanny about looking after Danny while I work." Caroline ignored Danny's audible groan.

"Top of the stairs, turn to the right. Knock on the double doors at the end of the hall."

Caroline thanked her and they left Trudie busily checking the buffet and coffeepots.

Danny hung back and grumbled all the way up the stairs.

"It's going to be fun," Caroline assured him. "Like daycare and preschool…only better. Just the two of you to play with all the toys."

"Girls' stuff," he muttered.

"Did you notice her cowboy boots and hat? And she has her own ponies." She smiled to herself as his frown disappeared.

"I guess she's okay."

"You'll have your own special teacher, too. Felicia seems very nice. And this afternoon we'll go horseback riding—if you behave yourself." She wasn't above a little bit of bribery when the situation invited it.

She found Felicia's apartment on the second floor at the opposite end from their rooms. She knocked on the double doors. It opened slowly and Cassie peeked out. Her round eyes instantly fixed on Danny. "What do you want?"

"May we come in?" Caroline asked politely, ignoring the two children glaring at each other.

"We've already had breakfast," Cassie declared with obvious satisfaction as she opened the door wider. "You can't be sleepy-heads and eat with us."

"We already ate," Danny declared trium-phantly.

The apartment's sitting room was quite spacious and light with the morning sun pouring through windows along one wall. Draperies, furniture throws and fringed gaudy lamps were various shades of red and purple. Artificial flowers were displayed on small tables covered with silk cloths and Caroline could smell an invading scent of potpourri coming from a cut-glass bowl.

Cassie pranced ahead of them into an adjoining room which was obviously the playroom of a very rich little girl. Even Danny's eyes widened as he looked around at the games, toys, paints, clay and inviting electronic gadgets he'd only seen in toy stores.

Cassie knocked on one of the doors at the far side of the room and called out loudly, "That boy's here."

The bedroom door opened almost immediately and Felicia glided into the room wearing a long multicolored robe that swept the floor. Her salt-and-pepper hair was held back by a braided band and fell freely halfway down her back. If Felicia was embarrassed by her less-than-formal appearance, there was no evidence of it.

"I hope we're not too early," Caroline quickly apologized.

"Not at all," she said smiling and in a formal tone, she said, "Good morning, Danny."

To Caroline's surprise, Danny responded with a preschool ritual. "Good morning, Miss...Miss..." He fumbled for the right name.

"Felicia. Fe...lis...e...a," she pronounced phonetically. When he repeated it, she nodded. "Very good."

Danny beamed. Caroline began to relax.

"Cassie, why don't you set up the race track for you and Danny? And let him have his choice of cars?" she prompted.

The car-racing game must have been a rare treat because Cassie's frown instantly changed in to a wide smile. Caroline blessed Felicia for recognizing a pivotal moment and handling it so beautifully. The two children happily busied themselves setting up the track and positioning their choice of cars.

"Would you join me in a second cup of coffee

while the children get acquainted a bit?" Felicia asked Caroline.

"Yes, thank you." She doubted that Stella would be looking for her this early.

Felicia motioned toward the kitchenette. A small round table and chairs were in an alcove off the main room. Caroline didn't see any dishes in the sink or on the table.

"You must have breakfast early," she commented as Felicia brought cups and a coffeepot from an apartment-sized stove over to the table.

"Dawn is the best time to greet the world. Vibrations are at their highest then. All shadows of the night flee before the healing rays of the sun, you know," she said as she sat down opposite Caroline. "Of course, Cassie wakes up several hours later."

Caroline took a sip of coffee before responding to her unusual remarks. "I can imagine how a person could lose oneself in the grandeur of the surroundings. You must love being here."

"I'm always ready to go back to sunbaked earth, clear skies and warm nights. Texas is home."

"Have you lived there all your life?"

She nodded. "My parents worked on Wes's grandfather's ranch when they first came over the border. I grew up there. Sadly, Wes lost both of his parents while he was still in college but when he got married, he asked me to come and work for him."

Caroline wanted to know how she had liked Wes's wife, but she refrained from asking. Gossiping with the nanny wasn't exactly the wisest thing to do.

"I really appreciate your looking after Danny."

Felicia's forehead was suddenly creased with thoughtful lines. She didn't answer as she stirred her coffee.

She doesn't want to do it. Now what?

"Danny really isn't as difficult to handle as he might appear," Caroline quickly assured

Felicia. "He has a lot of interests and he wouldn't demand a lot of time if he has something to do."

Felicia set down her spoon and sighed deeply. "It isn't that. He's a fine little boy, I can tell that."

"Then what?"

"Nothing," she said but her eyes betrayed her words. There was a haunted look about them.

Caroline was suddenly uneasy. She'd leave the lodge in a minute if she felt it wasn't safe leaving Danny in this woman's care.

"If there's something that might affect my son, I need to know it now. Tell me."

Felicia took another sip of her coffee, carefully holding the cup steady with both hands. Then, slowly, she set it down and took a deep breath.

"I'll let no harm come to your boy, I promise."

Whatever reservation Felicia had had in her own mind seemed to be resolved. In the weighted silence, they could hear the children squealing in the other room. Danny was cheering and Cassie was laughing deeply.

"It will be good for them to be playmates," Felicia said as she reached across and patted Caroline's hand. "You do your work and I will take good care of your son, I promise. I have taken care of Cassie since she was born. They trust me and so should you." Her dark eyes hardened. "You pay no attention to what anyone says. Today is not yesterday."

Caroline wasn't sure what Felicia meant by that cryptic remark, but she knew that she wouldn't rest easy until she found out.

Chapter Four

Caroline left Danny sitting on the floor, watching as a red racer careened around a track. He barely gave his mother a quick glance as she said, "I'm leaving now, Danny. You stay here with Cassie and Felicia."

"Okay." His face was flushed and his eyes bright. "I'm ahead of Cassie two laps."

"You're going to miss a curve going that fast," Cassie retorted as if she'd learned that lesson the hard way. "Wait and see! Then I'll catch up."

"No, you won't."

Felicia gave Caroline a reassuring smile as she eased down in a nearby chair and picked up her sewing basket.

"I'll be back before lunch," Caroline said. Everything seemed to be under control. She couldn't find any rational reason for a lingering apprehension. *Quit being an overprotective mother,* she told herself, but the lecture didn't do much good. She wished they'd never left home.

Her chest tightened. *What home?*

After leaving Felicia's apartment, she walked the length of the hall to her rooms and spent a few minutes making up the beds and putting things away. Because of her limited finances, she'd shopped for only enough clothes for about a week. One of her first challenges would be to find the laundry room.

After glancing at her watch, she decided she'd go downstairs and see if Stella was ready to give her the tour of the lodge that she'd promised and tell her what rooms she wanted redone.

The eating room was empty except for Trudie Benson who was clearing off the buffet. When Caroline asked about Stella, she nodded.

"She had breakfast and I think she left to talk to Tim Henderson. He's the year-round manager-caretaker, you know."

Caroline remembered that Wes has mentioned Tim before.

"Well, you'll probably find them in his office. It's just down the hall at the back of the house. It has an outside entrance so Tim can come and go without having to traipse through the whole house. He spends half his time outside checking the property and overseeing the two stablemen.

"Maybe I shouldn't bother them."

Trudie waved away the objection with her chubby hand. "Tim doesn't stand on ceremony. Besides, if Stella isn't there, he'll probably know where she is."

Trudie's instructions seemed simple enough, but Caroline soon discovered that the hall didn't continue in a straight line but made several abrupt turns. She passed a couple of narrow stairways rising to the floor above. She hugged herself against a penetrating chill in the dank, shadowy hall. The only sound was her own steps vibrating on the planked floor.

When the silence was broken by a floating echo of Stella's laughter, Caroline let out a breath of relief. Quickening her steps, she reached a door that opened into a low-ceilinged room with one window and an outside door. The furnishings were meager: a desk, a couple of straight-back chairs and some gray metal file cabinets.

A muscular man of about forty, with a weathered face and sandy hair was half sitting on the corner of the old desk and smiling at Stella who stood close by.

Both turned quickly in Caroline's direction when she appeared in the doorway. From their startled expressions she couldn't tell whether she'd interrupted something personal or they were just surprised to see her.

Stella waved her in. "Come and meet Tim Henderson. He's the boss around here."

"Hardly," he objected with an easy smile.

"I told you about her, Caroline Fairchild. She's the decorator who's going to help me put a little class in this place. And about time, too," Stella added as if she'd fought more than one battle on this subject.

"Welcome to Shadow Mountain," he said, shaking her hand. From his slight Western drawl, Caroline assumed he was another Texan. "Reckon you gals are going to be pretty busy, all right."

"You better believe it. Maybe we'll start here." Stella gave him a teasing smile as she glanced around the packed office.

"Not on your life, honey."

"Oh, you men. Wes has already warned us to leave his suite and the gun room alone. You'll be sorry when you see how beautiful the rest of the lodge turns out." She turned to Caroline. "I'll show you the lodge and we can decide where we'll start first."

Tim walked with them to the hall door. "I hope you can keep a rein on this gal. She can be a handful sometimes."

Caroline wondered if he was speaking from experience.

As they walked down the hall, Stella explained, "We have our own generator, water supply and telephone service via Telluride. Cell phones are useless here. And no house mail delivery. We order groceries from Telluride or go after them ourselves."

As they toured the main floor, Caroline was thoroughly frustrated with Stella's ambivalence about making any decisions about basic changes she wanted. They could end up with a hodgepodge of fabrics, colors and furnishings that completely lacked harmony and balance.

Caroline was ready to call a halt to the unorganized approach and suggested they spend the afternoon going over some basic plans.

"Oh, I can't," Stella said. "You're on your own

for the rest of the day. We'll get together again tomorrow morning and go over some ideas."

Caroline swallowed back a protest. A myriad of initial decisions had to be made before they could proceed. Spending only half days working out the details could extend the project almost indefinitely.

Caroline would have made an issue of the matter if she hadn't already agreed to spend the late afternoon with Wes and the children.

"I'll show you the workroom and you can get set up there," Stella said as if she sensed Caroline's impatience. "I've made a collection of magazines, books and articles that offer some good suggestions. You could look them over and see what you think."

"That might be a place to start," Caroline agreed.

When Stella showed her the workroom and Caroline saw the pile of material stacked on a long work table, she silently groaned. It would take more than one day to go through that collection.

"I set up my laptop and printer." Stella motioned to a small table. "I thought that would be an easy way for you to make some notes. Anything else?" she asked.

"No, that's fine," Caroline lied. The woman hadn't given her any clues about what she had in mind nor any specific changes she wished to make in any of the rooms. Caroline was thoroughly frustrated. If Stella had already decided on some definite ideas, this would be the time to share them, but she left Caroline alone in the workroom without another word.

As Caroline sifted though a pile of books and a dozen magazines, all new, she didn't see any signs that Stella had gone through them. Usually clients marked specific ideas that they liked or turned down pages for easy reference.

Caroline leaned back in her chair, suddenly

overwhelmed by the project ahead. How could she hope to please Stella when she didn't have a clue how to begin to shape her nebulous ideas?

When she left the workroom and returned to Felicia's apartment, Danny and Cassie were happily playing with clay. If her son had missed her, there was no outward sign of it.

"Time to go downstairs for lunch," she told him.

"I don't like that stuffy old dining room," Cassie said, wrinkling up her pert nose.

"Me, neither," Danny echoed.

"Why don't I fix the children something here?" Felicia offered.

"Yay," they said, almost in unison.

Caroline laughed. "All right. I'll be back after lunch to get you for your nap, Danny."

When he groaned, she reminded him that they were going horseback-riding later in the afternoon.

"Oh, I forgot."

"I don't want you to fall asleep on Cassie's pony."

"Blackie will keep him awake," Cassie promised with a grin.

On the way downstairs, Caroline realized she would much rather have stayed and had lunch with the kids. When she reached the dining room, she was even more regretful.

Dexter was the only one there. He was wearing burgundy leather pants and a plaid shirt that only emphasized his beefy build and pot belly.

"Hi there, pretty lady," he greeted her as she came in, immediately rising to his feet. He stayed at her elbow while she selected soup and salad from the buffet and then ushered her over to the table where he was sitting.

"Where's Wes?" she asked pointedly as he guided her chair to the table.

"Oh, he's holed up in his suite, working. The price of being rich, I guess. He has to keep on top of things no matter where he goes. No rest for the weary—or the rich," he added, grinning. "Wes has probably talked to a dozen big shots this morning, keeping the wheels of commerce moving, you know." His tone was tinged with something that might have been jealousy.

"It's too bad he can't relax when he's here," Caroline said, already impatient with the man's boorish manner.

"Oh, I think he does. This lodge has really been a godsend. It's one of the blessings his grandfather left the family. I doubt that Wes or his father would have built it. When his parents died Wes inherited all the family property and fortune held in escrow for the oldest living male Wainwright." Dexter gave Caroline a knowing wink. "Wes is quite a catch for any gal who plays her cards right."

Caroline forced herself to say lightly, "I imagine there are plenty of downsides. How many times has he been married?"

"Just once. He married a Texas beauty

queen, Pamela Labesky. Wow, that gal could send any man's desire into orbit just looking at her. She was something else and once Pamela set her silver tiara for Wes, he didn't have a chance. Ruined him for any other woman, that's for sure." Dexter looked thoughtful as he speared a link sausage and popped it in his mouth. "Too bad Pamela only enjoyed her good fortune and Wainwright prestige for a few years. You know about the plane crash?"

"Only that Stella said she lost her husband in one."

"The same crash. Wes would have been with them if something hadn't come up at the last minute to keep him in Houston. Stella and Shane were already at the lodge. Wes pilots his own plane, you know. Anyway, Delvin and Pamela decided not to wait for him and they hired a pilot to fly them to Colorado. Bad decision. There's a dangerous downdraft when landing in these mountains. The pilot miscalculated."

"How awful."

"Wes took it pretty hard. The tragedy was tough on him, that's for sure."

"How long ago was that?'

"Cassie was only a few months old when the plane crashed. And then there was—" He broke off as Shane came into the room.

Apparently Dexter preferred gossiping when no one else was around. He quickly changed the subject and asked Caroline how the redecorating was going.

She made a non-committal answer then purposefully gave her full attention to her lunch.

Shane made no attempt to join them and slumped down at a window table by himself. He had the stand-offish air of an adolescent and the common belligerency that went along with it. Caroline finished her lunch as quickly as possible and wasn't pleased when Dexter left the dining room with her.

"Why don't you let me show you around the place?" he offered, trying to take her arm. "You haven't been down to the stables yet, have you?"

"The children and I are going riding with Wes this afternoon," she told him quickly. "I'm looking forward to it."

"I bet you are," he said with a slight smirk. "All the women enjoy Wes's company."

She refrained from making a caustic reply about his own apparent lack of charm in that area. Being trapped under the same roof with him was going to test her endurance for repulsive men. If Wes left the lodge, she hoped to heaven he took Dexter Tate with him.

AFTER A LONG NAP, Caroline and Danny made their way down to the social room to meet Wes. She'd changed into jeans and the bright sweater she'd worn the night before. Danny wore a pair of new overalls and a denim jacket. She was glad she'd invested in boots for both of them.

The social room was empty. No sign of Wes nor of Cassie. Caroline felt an instant pang of disappointment. Maybe something had come up and Wes had changed his mind—or he'd forgotten.

No, Cassie wouldn't let him forget, Caroline decided. Not that willful little girl. Thank heavens she and Danny seemed to have taken to each other—at least for the moment.

As the minutes passed, she was beginning to think he'd completely forgotten their date when she heard Cassie's high-pitched chatter floating down the hall.

Caroline smiled at Danny. "Here they come."

The little girl darted into the room ahead of Wes. She was dressed like a movie-star rodeo queen. White fringed pants matched a fringed studded vest and white boots. Her cowboy hat was the same shade of red as her satin shirt.

She grinned from ear to ear as she put one hand on her hip and demanded, "Well, what do you think?"

Danny missed the nature of her question. "I think you're late."

"Spoken like a true man," Wes said, chuckling. "Sorry, I got held up by a telephone call. Anyway, I sent word ahead to the stable. The horses should be saddled up and waiting."

Cassie danced ahead of them down a worn path under a canopy of ponderosa pine trees. Danny followed at her heels. Wes fell into step beside Caroline and she realized that she was nervous and rather ill at ease.

Maybe she'd given him the wrong idea about her riding ability? After all, a farm horse wasn't in the same league as a prancing thoroughbred. What if she made a complete fool of herself?

At that moment, she realized how much she wanted to impress this rich, handsome Texan.

Why, she didn't know. In a few days he'd be gone and most likely she'd never see him again. Still, her feminine vanity wanted him to remember her as a capable horseback rider.

When they reached the stable her misgivings were doubled. Wes nodded toward a restless sorrel mare all saddled up and tethered beside two small shaggy ponies, one black and one dark brown. Two middle-aged stablehands nodded at Wes and then went about their business in the barn.

Cassie immediately ran over to the ponies. "You can ride Blackie," she informed Danny. "He's kinda old. I like Cocoa best."

"They're both gentle," Wes quickly assured Caroline. "We bought them from a Texas breeder who specializes in Shetland ponies. They're a good mount for children. Strong and muscular, but rein-easy."

Caroline began to relax. The saddles, harnesses and stirrups were proportionate to the size of a small rider. This could be a wonderful chance for her son to experience his first horseback ride.

"I'll walk along beside Danny," Wes told her. "We'll follow the path around to the western end of the lake. You can ride ahead if you'd like and we'll catch up with you."

"Why don't I walk with Danny and you ride?"

"Because I want you to enjoy yourself," he replied flatly and his tone brooked no argument.

He cupped his hands and helped Cassie up into the saddle. As she took the reins in her little hands, she grinned at Danny. "Race you to the lake."

"Cassie! We'll have none of that," Wes said sharply and quickly helped wide-eyed Danny mount the other pony. "I'll keep the reins for a while, Danny," he said reassuringly. "We'll just go for a nice walk."

As Caroline led the sorrel mare out of the barn, Wes watched. There was an easy, confident stride in her movement that pleased him. Nothing about her was showy or pretentious. Deftly she arrange the reins in her hands and patted the mare's neck. As Wes watched her swing easily into the saddle, he smiled to himself.

She hadn't lied. She settled back in the saddle as if she were born to it.

Maybe they could go for a real ride before he left, he mused. He'd like to take her up one of the rugged trails and show her God's country from the top of a mountain ridge.

The path down to the lake was a twisting one, weaving in and out of thick stands of pine and spruces. Caroline and Cassie rode ahead while Wes walked in front of Danny's pony, leading it at a comfortable pace.

When they broke out of the trees at the edge of a meadow slanting down to the water, he stopped and handed Danny the reins.

"I'll stay by the horse's head while you guide him," he told the wide-eyed boy. "You hold the reins like this," he instructed as he put them in Danny's hands. "Now, when you pull back on them and say whoa, that tells Blackie you want to stop. Understand?"

Danny nodded his head vigorously.

"Okay. Now when you move the reins to this side and tighten them that turns his head and Blackie goes in that direction. When you put them on the other side he turns that way. Got it?"

Danny grinned and nodded.

"Good. Now give him a little kick and say geddy-up."

Wes smothered a chuckle at Danny's croaky little voice and his wide-eyed look as the pony moved forward. Looking at the shine on his little face tightened Wes's chest. Suddenly he was filled with an unexpected resentment that fate had cheated him of having a son to raise. He loved his little daughter with all his heart, but a son would have had a special place in his life. Watching him grow into manhood and take over the Wainwright financial holdings would have made all the challenges worthwhile.

"This is fun," Danny said, his eyes sparkling and his mouth curved in a broad smile.

"You're a real cowboy now," Wes told him, chuckling at the boy's enthusiasm.

As they reached the lake, he could tell that Caroline was anxious when she saw her son with the reins in his hands. Her short wavy hair was windblown and her face ruddy from the ride. Wes was all too aware of the way her slender body hugged the rounded contours of the horse.

As Danny reached her, he reined in his horse with a forceful, "Whoa!"

She laughed with such abandonment that Wes found himself laughing with her.

"You want to race?" Cassie challenged.

"Sure," Danny answered promptly with all the false confidence of a beginner.

"No way!" Wes said firmly. He pointed to a grassy knoll a short distance away. "Caroline, there's a nice view of the lake and alpine meadow from there. Shall we leave the horses here and take a look?"

Her smile was nearly as broad as her son's. "Yes, I'd like that."

Caroline quickly dismounted and tethered her mount to a nearby tree while Wes helped the children.

THE CHILDREN scampered like young goats up a slope of rocks that flattened out in a natural lookout above the lake. As Caroline and Wes followed, she was surprised he reached out and took her hand when they reached a rather steep mound of boulders. His clasp was firm and he kept his supple fingers interlaced with hers all the way to the top of the ridge.

She suddenly realized how much she'd missed sharing the simplest joys with someone else. Her son had become her whole life and she'd lost a part of herself just taking care of him and managing the necessities of life.

Nothing in Wes's manner was the least bit flirtatious and she chided herself for the warmth that flowed through her from his touch. She even toyed with the idea of missing a step just to see if he'd catch her. He radiated the kind of sensuality and masculine virility that made her feel utterly feminine.

He quickly dropped her hand when they reached the high plateau where the children were running wildly about near a drop-off ledge.

"Stop that!" he ordered in a no-nonsense tone. He motioned to a pile of flat stones a safe distance from the edge. "Sit down over there."

Cassie scampered over to the spot but Danny hung back.

Caroline could tell from her son's stubborn frown he was debating whether or not he had to obey Cassie's father.

Wes continued to watch him without saying

anything more. Very slowly Danny shuffled his feet and moved over to the rocks where Cassie was sitting.

Wes turned around and as he winked at Caroline, she smothered a smile.

They walked over and joined the children. As the sun was beginning to set behind a high craggy mountain range, they made their way back down to the lake and the horses.

Caroline held out the reins of the mare to him. "You ride and I'll walk."

The way she took charge totally surprised him. Nobody flatly gave him orders. He'd grown up with the conviction that people should and would do his bidding whenever he expressed his wishes. Her steady unwavering look was one he wasn't used to seeing and there wasn't the slightest hint that she was open to negotiation. He decided to let her think he was amiable to her dictates—for now.

He let Cassie lead the way back on her pony.

Caroline came next, walking beside Danny's horse.

Wes followed on the sorrel mare, riding close enough to handle the unexpected if Danny suddenly lost control of the animal.

The Rocky Mountains were a treacherous playground. Unexpected threats like snakes and wild animals could send the most placid horse into a frenzy without warning. Even the most docile mount could get spooked by a situation that couldn't be anticipated.

Wes felt a swell of protectiveness and suddenly realized this woman and her son had engaged his emotions on a level that was both foolhardy and dangerous.

People he deeply cared about always seemed to end up dead.

Chapter Five

When they returned to the lodge, Wes suggested the four of them have dinner in his suite.

"That would be nice," Caroline replied, totally surprised. The thought of eating with Dexter, Stella and the others made acceptance easy.

"Goody." Cassie clapped. "Can we have a picnic? It's fun," she told Danny. "We sit on the floor and eat."

"Sorry, not tonight, Cassie," Wes said. "We'll sit at a table and mind our manners."

She puckered her lower lip. Danny frowned as if he didn't think much of Wes's idea either. Obviously, minding their manners was not high on either of the children's lists.

Caroline would have voted for the picnic herself. Her experience dining in private suites with the wealthy was lacking.

"My rooms are in the west wing of the lodge, second floor at the end of the hall," Wes told her. "Shall we say six? I think Felicia likes to get Cassie to bed by eight."

"Sometimes I stay up 'til nine," Danny bragged in a tone that challenged Cassie's early hour.

"Me, too," the little girl quickly retorted. "Sometimes ten and eleven—"

"That's enough." Wes chuckled, obviously amused that the two of them were trying to upstage each other. "Maybe we can put both of you to bed early. What do you think, Caroline? Shall we plan some quiet time for ourselves?"

He'd never used that tone before and she didn't know what he was really asking. Was there a double meaning in the question? The thought crossed her mind that this whole dinner invitation might be only a smooth come-on. Rich, handsome and sexy, no doubt Wes Wainwright was used to having women fawn over him. Maybe she'd been sending the wrong signals? *Get rid of the kids and then what?* she wanted to ask. Even though his manner was totally friendly and seemed quite innocent, she was suspicious.

"All this fresh air and exercise will make me ready for an early bedtime, too," she replied quickly.

Later, when she had time to think about it, she suspected that she was flattering herself even thinking Wesley Wainwright might want to amuse himself with her company. He'd probably asked her to dinner because he was bored and, perhaps, wanted to avoid the others downstairs as much as she did.

AT SIX O'CLOCK, Wes answered Caroline's knock on the suite's door. He was pleased that she was punctual. He hated being kept waiting and his usual experience with women sorely tested his patience in that respect.

"Are they here?" Cassie asked, running to the door.

Felicia had brought her up to the suite a few minutes earlier. "I'll wait up," she had told him.

"It won't be late. We'll all be turning in early."

He was a little chagrined that his suggestion of extending the evening beyond the children's bedtime had met with negative vibes from the attractive Ms. Fairchild. He couldn't remember when his offer to spend time with an attractive woman had been turned down. Apparently, he'd been too obvious about wanting to spend time with her without the kids.

Cassie looked quite the sweet, little princess with her hair hanging loose behind a pink ribbon, but a mischievous sparkle in her eyes warned him to keep a tight rein on her.

A subtle rivalry was quite evident between

the two youngsters. It amused him the way they challenged each other. Having Danny around would be good for Cassie. She'd always had things go her way without any competition from someone her own age.

Trudie had sent up two barbecued beef dinners and two baked chicken meals, complete with drinks and apple tarts for dessert.

"Smells good," Caroline said, smiling.

"Me and Danny are having chicken," Cassie piped up. "And there's dessert." Then she whispered audibly to Danny. "Ask for two apple tarts. They're good. I snuck a bite."

"That's my daughter." Wes shook his head. "Danny, we'll have to make sure she gets the one with the bite out of it."

Danny giggled.

Caroline had changed into simple black slacks and a tailored white knitted sweater. He was glad he'd decided on tan cords and a casual dark green turtleneck pullover. Obviously, Caroline Fairchild wasn't a fancy dresser, but he could imagine a short party skirt swirling around those slim hips and long legs.

"Everything's ready," he said and motioned them into the spacious room where an expanse of windows framed a view of Shadow Mountain's craggy peak.

A night owl's lamenting cry sounded from a high perch in a ponderosa tree brushing its needled branches against the outside walls of the lodge. Twilight had already settled in the high valley and only the reflection of lights from the lodge lessened the invading darkness outside.

"Have a seat," Wes said, waving his hand toward a table that had been set for four at one end of the large room. "I'll bring in the food."

"Can I help?"

"Nope. But I could suggest a tip if the service is good," he quipped and winked suggestively.

When her cheeks flushed slightly, he realized she wasn't used to these kinds of glib sexual innuendoes. He'd been around uninhibited, anything-goes women for so long, he'd forgotten there were other kinds.

Caroline was surprised how relaxed she felt when they'd finished eating and all moved into the living room. Wes fixed a Scotch and soda for himself and a cream Kahlua for her.

Cassie went immediately to a large built-in cupboard and opened a bottom drawer. Impatiently, the little girl fished through a pile of toys until she found the game she wanted. Then she plopped down on the rug and motioned for Danny to join her.

As Cassie opened up a game board and set it between them, Caroline was surprised to see that it was a preschool Scrabble game. Although Danny had learned to read some simple words while watching *Sesame Street* and recognized beginning sounds, Caroline wasn't sure he was up to playing that kind of word game. She kept her eye on him as Cassie dealt out the letter tiles.

Wes must have picked up on her concern. "Don't worry. Cassie will play for both of them," he assured her. "She's not competitive about winning and she's used to Felicia helping her read words she doesn't know."

"I wish I'd had more time to work with Danny this past year," Caroline said regretfully, but much to her surprise Danny did very well.

When his score inched higher than Cassie's, he gave his mother a huge grin. She smiled back and gave him a thumbs-up sign.

"I envy you," Wes said and his tone made her look at him.

He was watching at Danny and his expression betrayed a deep emotion she hadn't seen before. She was startled by the sudden pain in his eyes. "I lost my son. He was just an infant, a month old. I never got to know him."

"Oh, I'm so sorry," Caroline said quickly.

His expression hardened and suddenly the set

of his jaw spoke of a consuming anger. For the first time Caroline was aware of underlying fury behind his smooth, controlled manner. He was obviously still hurting and angry at a fate that had deprived him of his son. After taking a deep drink of his Scotch and soda, he put down the empty glass with a punctuating sound.

She was at a loss how to respond. Probing questions about his grief were not appropriate. For several minutes he visibly retreated into a private agony of his own and the children's chatter and laughter were the only sounds in the room.

She was uncomfortable in his strained silence and searched for something to say, but everything seemed too light and inappropriate in the face of his deep emotional turmoil.

When the children put aside the game and Cassie pestered Wes for another apple tart, he seemed to shake off his mood and assume his role of the genial host.

When Felicia came to collect Cassie, Caroline decided it was time for them to go, too.

"I'm sorry," he apologized as he walked them to the door. "I'm afraid I haven't been at my best tonight. Sometimes the past catches up with me."

She nodded. "I understand." She couldn't even begin to imagine what it would feel like to lose her precious Danny.

CAROLINE DIDN'T SEE WES at all the next day and spent most of her time going over the decorating books and magazines in the workroom.

Stella popped in from time to time, but Caroline's frustration grew. Despite all their conversations, nothing seemed to be moving them toward any concrete decisions.

Try as she would, Caroline failed to get a feel for Stella's overall intentions for the lodge. Was the woman only going to redecorate on a superficial level or was she thinking of making some basic changes—like combining some of the small rooms into larger living areas?

Caroline was puzzled. Even though Wes had apparently given Stella free rein to carry out her project, Caroline sensed a hesitation in the woman to act on her own. Perhaps she'd seen that angry, brooding side of her brother-in-law often enough to be wary.

Caroline was uneasy herself about seeing Wes again. Behind that easy smile of his, she'd glimpsed a tortured spirit. She was tempted to ask Stella for the particulars around the loss of Wes's son, but keeping everything on a business footing was important, especially while they lived under the same roof.

Late that afternoon, she received a telephone call from the Denver fire chief that put everything else out of her mind; he told her that their investigation had determined beyond a doubt that her house fire was definitely arson.

"We found empty containers of a flammable

liquid in the alley and two broken windows in the basement, where the fire started."

"I can't believe it!"

"Do you know of anyone who would deliberately want to burn your house down and hurt you, Mrs. Fairchild?"

She was stunned by the question.

"No…no one…" she choked.

"Maybe an old enemy of your husband's? I understand he was a doctor. Maybe a former patient of his went off his rocker and wanted to get even."

"My husband has been dead for four years. Why would anyone wait until now—"

"Who knows?" he answered shortly. "The fact is someone set the fire for a reason. I understand you have full fire coverage on the house and contents."

"Yes."

"A rather extensive policy. In cases like this, the homeowner comes under intense scrutiny."

"I did not burn down my own house," Caroline flared angrily. "And the police had better spend their time finding out who did."

"I'm sure you'll be hearing from them as the investigation proceeds. Are you going to remain at your present location for some time? If not, you should advise them of your whereabouts."

Caroline hung up the phone and brushed a hand across her forehead as she muttered, "I can't believe this."

"Bad news?"

She jerked her head up. Dexter was standing close to the alcove where the telephone was located on the main floor. She hadn't heard him come up behind her.

"Can I help?"

He certainly wasn't the person she would have chosen to unload on, but her exasperation made her explode. "They think I burned down my house for the insurance."

"Who's they?"

"The Denver police and fire department."

He let out a low whistle. "Well, I guess it happens like that sometimes. I mean, I've known cases—"

She brushed by him and headed up the stairs. If Dexter had followed her, glibly chattering, she might have happily tripped him.

Once inside her bedroom, she sat on the edge of the bed and stared at the floor. As she went over and over the telephone conversation, she tried to make some sense of it. The fact that someone had set the fire was a total shock, but having the suspicion fall on her was a double blow. She was angry and sick to her stomach at the same time.

Who could have done it?

She didn't believe for a minute that it had been an ex-patient of her husband. If anything, Thomas had been too concerned about every one of them. She couldn't think of a single case where there had been any kind of incident that would warrant revenge.

There had been some petty destruction in her neighborhood from time to time, but mostly kids' stuff. Nothing even as serious as broken car windows.

Pressing her fingers against her forehead, she struggled to make sense out of everything. It had to be vandals! A high school was only a few blocks away. Undoubtedly, the police would look there first. The arson could be gang-related. She'd heard of gang initiations where the newcomer had to prove his worth in order to join the group. Some hopeful could have been trying to show he was good enough to be in the gang.

As this thought took hold, the tension inside her began to ease. She went into the bathroom and after splashing her face with warm water and combing her hair, she straightened her shoulders and glanced at her watch.

Time to pick up Danny.

Felicia's door was open and the two children were playing some kind of treasure-hunt game and darting all over the apartment and the hall, looking for clues. Danny's were written in blue and Cassie's in red.

Felicia had cleverly used the primer words they knew and drawn pictures to illustrate hiding places like a kitchen chair, a sofa pillow, a clock or cooking utensils. One clue led them to another and Caroline and Felicia laughed as they watched them racing to see who could find their treasure first.

Luckily, they both found their candy bars within seconds of each other. Cassie's was hidden behind a photograph and Danny's prize was inside the cookie jar.

"Good job," Caroline told both of them and complimented Felicia on her ingenuity. "What a great way to improve their reading skills. You're a wonderful teacher."

Felicia flushed as if she wasn't used to such compliments and quickly changed the subject. "I have some lemonade ready for the children. Would you like a cup of tea?"

"I'd love one," Caroline said honestly.

Danny's face glowed as he bit into his chocolate bar and his brown eyes sparkled with childish glee. A warm feeling poured over Caroline as she watched him. As long as her son was happy and safe, she could cope with anything.

While the children watched a cartoon video, the two women had some privacy in the breakfast nook. Caroline was never quite sure afterwards how the conversation had led around to Wes Wainwright, but found herself saying, "I was shocked when he told me about the tragic loss of his son."

Felicia set down her teacup with such force that the liquid spilled onto the table. Her eyes rounded. "He told you?"

"Yes, last night, when we had dinner in his suite."

Her dark eyes fixed on Caroline like someone waiting for an ax to fall. Her voice was ragged and her breath short. "He told you—everything?"

"Only that he'd lost an infant son. He didn't go into details but I could tell that he was still mourning the baby's death. What happened? How did he die?"

Caroline thought Felicia was going to leave the table without replying. Then she straightened her back and her eyes were moist as she pleaded, "You have to understand. It wasn't my fault. Everyone said it wasn't."

Felicia suddenly looked as tortured as Wes had the night before. Caroline wasn't sure she wanted to hear any more. The way the woman was defending herself indicated that she must have some guilt over the baby's death. But if Felicia was responsible in any way, why on earth would Wes have left Cassie in her care?

As quickly as she could, Caroline apologized for bringing up the subject. "I'm sorry, I didn't realize you suffered the infant's untimely death as well as the family. It's always traumatic to bury a baby."

"That's what makes it so awful." Felicia swallowed hard. "We didn't even have a baby to bury."

"I don't understand."

She sobbed, "Cassie was a twin. She had a twin brother. They were only a month old when it happened."

"What happened?"

"He was kidnapped."

Caroline felt as if someone had knocked the air out of her. In a strained voice, Felicia told Caroline how she'd taken a fussy Cassie to bed with her in a room adjoining the nursery. Near morning, when Felicia went to put Cassie back in her crib, the baby boy was gone. A demand for ransom was never made and all of the wealth and resources of the Wainwrights failed to find any trace of the kidnapped baby.

Felicia was crying now and Caroline bent over her, putting an arm around her shoulder. Her own mouth was dry and her chest tight.

Poor Wes. Her heart went out to him. And to Felicia. What an emotional burden for the two of them. Watching Cassie grow up must create a kind of never-ending torment for them.

If Felicia was really blameless…?

The thought was like a prick of barbed wire. If a baby had been kidnapped while it was under her care, could this woman really be trusted with Danny?

Chapter Six

When Caroline and Danny went downstairs for dinner, Stella and her son, Shane, were the only ones who came in while they were eating. Without an invitation, Stella sat down at their table and Shane followed. His pained look clearly indicated it wasn't his choice.

"I guess Wes and Dexter aren't back yet," Stella said. "They took the Jeep to Telluride to get some supplies."

Shane muttered audibly, "They probably ran out of beer."

"Maybe because someone else was helping them drink it," his mother countered sharply and added in a sarcastic tone, "I wonder who that might be."

Her son hunched over his plate without answering, but his scowl spoke volumes. Caroline shifted uncomfortably; she wasn't about to get involved in any family squabble.

Stella gave an exasperated sigh. "You give your life trying to make things good for your kid and what do you get? Nothing but grief. I found a half-dozen beer cans in Shane's room last night."

"The kind they show on TV?" Danny piped up. "You know, like those funny bears that laugh and sing?"

"I don't think Shane has a favorite," Stella answered coolly.

Caroline decided to take a sip of water and stay out of the conversation. A heavy silence followed, but the unspoken tension between Stella and her son was almost deafening.

Throughout the meal, it was obvious Stella

was in a very bad mood and Caroline decided it wasn't her role to make pleasant dinner conversation.

As soon as possible, she excused herself and made a hasty retreat with Danny out of the dining room.

Instead of going upstairs to their rooms, Caroline decided to check out a small reading room she'd noticed when Stella gave her a tour of the lodge.

"I want to go play with Cassie," Danny complained loudly.

"Not tonight," she said firmly as she took his hand and led him down the hall. Maybe she was being foolish, but she intended to seek some reassurance from Wes about Felicia. She needed to know that his confidence in letting Cassie remain under the nanny's supervision was well-founded.

The reading room wasn't a library by any means. It was a small, square room with a few bookcases offering a variety of reading material. Some straight chairs were placed around a small table and an uncomfortable-looking couch that looked like a discard from a garage sale stood against one wall.

Caroline was disappointed. The reading room completely lacked warmth and comfort. She hoped it was on Stella's list to redecorate.

Once again a feeling of frustration swept over her. If she'd had any other clients waiting, she might have pushed Stella to make some decisions but as it was, unfortunately, Caroline had more time than anything else at the moment.

She spied some books on one of the lower shelves and was delighted to find they were children's picture books as well as classes such as *The Little Engine That Could* and *Are You My Mother?*

Danny grabbed them as if they were familiar friends. She smiled as he sat on the couch and eagerly turned the pages. Her trips to the library with him had paid off. She'd bet he was going to be a reader just like her.

She quickly surveyed the bookcases to see what she could find for herself. There were lots of books about wildlife, mountain-climbing and outdoor adventures.

Someone had made a collection of Westerns by Zane Grey and Louis L'Amour and she selected a couple of them to try. After all, when in Rome…

"Let's take the books up to our room, Danny. We can always come back down for more," she assured him.

As they were heading for the main staircase, Caroline heard Wes's voice at the front door. "Dexter, drive the Jeep around back. Tim will help you unload."

Caroline hesitated, trying to decide whether to go on up the stairs or turn around. He solved the problem for her.

"Hello there," he called as he hurried to catch

up with her. "We just got back from Telluride. We're later than I planned. Dexter had an agenda of his own, as always. That guy seems to collect buddies everywhere he goes. Anyway, we had dinner earlier. Did you have a good day?"

"Pleasant enough," she answered, sidestepping an honest answer. Complaining to him about Stella wasn't going to do any good. He'd already washed his hands of the whole decorating project.

"What about you, Danny?" Wes asked, putting his hand on the boy's shoulder as they mounted the stairs. "What have you got there?"

"Books. I can read 'em, too," he bragged. "Just like Cassie."

"I bet you can." Wes winked at Caroline. "Nothing like a little competition to speed things up. Did the two of them behave themselves today?"

She nodded. "Felicia had made a clever

treasure hunt game for them. They ran all over the apartment looking for clues—"

"And I found my candy bar in the cookie jar," bragged Danny.

"Felicia is always thinking up creative, fun games. It's a good thing, too." He sighed. "I know Cassie is a challenge to her sometimes. I'm afraid my daughter's going to be a terror when she starts regular school."

"Has Felicia always been Cassie's nanny?" Caroline asked, a little ashamed of herself for trying to verify Felicia's sad story. She couldn't see Wes's eyes clearly in the dim light, but she thought there was a tightening at the corners of his mouth.

"Yes. She'd been employed by my late wife's family and when Pamela was expecting, Felicia came to live with us. I don't know how I would have managed Cassie as a single parent without her. Are you concerned about leaving Danny with her?"

"A little."

"Don't be," he said flatly. "There have never been any questions about her loyalty. Your son is safe with her."

Like your son was?

It was all she could do to keep from plying him with questions about the kidnapping. Remembering how intensely he'd been discussing his loss, she hesitated to bring up the subject. If he trusted Felicia with his only child, what more reassurance did she need?

"Would you like to go riding tomorrow afternoon?"

Surprised, she stammered, "Oh, I…I don't know—"

"We ought to take advantage of the nice weather before we get hit with winter and socked in with five-foot snowdrifts.

"You mean we might get snowbound in October?"

"It's been known to happen. Usually not this early, though," he reassured her. "Anyway, tomorrow's going to be chilly but clear. A great day for a horseback ride. What do you say?"

Danny piped up, "I'll go."

Caroline laughed. "Not this time, honey."

"Is that a yes?" Wes asked. The way he searched her face seemed at odds with his usual air of assurance and command. "About three o'clock?"

The thought of enjoying a lovely horseback ride without the children was very tempting. When she was growing up on the farm she'd loved riding a galloping horse with the wind blowing her hair and the strong muscles of her mount rising and falling beneath her. How could she refuse an escape from the mounting pressures at the lodge?

"All right, if Stella doesn't object to a short workday."

"She won't," he flatly predicted. "Dress

warmly. We'll be heading up the canyon and the wind coming off the high ridges can be a little chilly."

To CAROLINE'S surprise, Stella informed her the next morning that she'd finally made some decisions.

"We'll start with the large main room."

"Good," Caroline replied, but her relief was short-lived; after asking Stella a few specific questions, she realized that the woman was still totally undecided about the effect she wanted to create.

They spent time discussing various options for minor renovations that would allow for more modern focus and design. They considered possible changes in furniture style, fabrics, wall hangings and floor coverings. Stella kept nodding as she listened to Caroline's advice, but continued to vacillate about making any definite selections. Caroline had the feeling she needed to be in charge but deep down didn't completely trust herself and would do anything to avoid admitting it.

By three o'clock Caroline was more than ready to escape the lodge. She'd been filled with a mixture of apprehension and excitement as she'd watched the clock all day.

It wasn't really anything like a date, she assured herself repeatedly. After her husband's death, even good friends like Betty and Jim had failed in their matchmaking efforts. She'd dated some very nice men but none of them had captured any serious interest. How ironic that she might finally be attracted to someone completely unavailable so far from home.

There wasn't any need for her to worry about what kind of an impression she might make. If there'd been any immediate feminine competition for his attention, she wouldn't be the one going horseback riding with a Texas tycoon.

She left Danny happily playing a video game

with Cassie while Felicia sat in her chair, knitting. She exchanged her slacks for jeans, put a denim jacket over a long-sleeved blouse and slipped into her new boots.

Hurrying down the stairs, she was surprised to find Wes waiting there for her. He was wearing brown Western pants, a matching shirt, a leather jacket, a narrow-brimmed Stetson and cowboy boots. She could tell from his expression he was trying to control his impatience.

"I'm sorry," she quickly apologized. "Leaving Danny took a few minutes longer than I'd planned."

He eyed what she was wearing and nodded as if he was satisfied she'd followed his advice. Then, to her surprise, handed her a lady's white Western hat.

"One of our guests left it at the lodge." He eyed the way it looked when she'd put it on. "Looks better on you."

"Was she blonde or brunette?" Caroline inquired with teasing solemnity.

"I guess it depends upon which day of the week we're talking about," he countered. "Shall we get out of here before I'm trapped by business?"

As they walked to the stables, he said, "I thought we'd head up the canyon to Cascade Falls. You ride well enough to hold to the trail. The view is spectacular. You shouldn't miss it while you're here."

His meaning was plain enough. This kind of outing wasn't on his usual busy agenda. Since this might be the one pleasant memory she took back to Denver, she was determined to enjoy it.

"It'll take us about thirty minutes to reach the falls," he told her. "If we're lucky the clouds will hold off until then. The view is unbelievable when the setting sun hits the water. It's one of my favorite rides."

The horses were saddled and waiting. Wes

nodded at the two stablemen. When he said something to them in Spanish, she realized they probably weren't fluent in English. She suspected he'd brought them here from his ranch in Texas.

Wes led the sorrel mare outside and held Caroline's stirrup as she lifted herself into the saddle. After she gathered the reins firmly in her hand, he went back in the stable and led out a black stallion.

"Beautiful!" Caroline exclaimed as the stallion raised dust with his prancing feet. "What's his name?"

"Prince."

"Fits him," Caroline readily replied.

"He was a wild one when we brought him in from the open range but we bonded from the beginning." Wes swung easily into the saddle and took command of the powerful animal with confidence.

Riding side by side, they passed the lake and

headed west across a meadow cupped by surrounding hillsides. When they came to a
narrow canyon bordered by high cliffs, Wes
reined his horse to a slow walk.

"We'll have to go single-file from here. Let
your mare have her footing. She'll follow Prince.
We can turn back now if you don't want to go any
farther. It's not going to be an easy—"

"Let's go," she said, interrupting him.
"Didn't you say we didn't have time to waste?"

He gave her an approving smile. "That's
what I thought."

As his stallion led the way up a rugged trail
cut into the side of a mountain, it seemed to
Caroline that they were climbing high enough
to reach the top of encircling peaks etched
across the skyline.

She heard the sound of rushing water even
before they reached Cascade Falls. As they
came through the trees, the ground leveled out
and alpine grass softened the rough gray

surface of a high precipice. They were only a short distance away from plunging cascades of white-foamed water falling from a rocky cliff high above.

After dismounting, they tied their mounts to trees whipped by the wind into grotesque shapes and walked to a spot which gave them a spectacular view of the falls.

Caroline caught her breath as cold mist sprayed their faces and a deafening roar rang in their ears. Streams of crystal water plunged hundreds of feet downward and then rose, spraying glistening gigantic boulders that lay below.

Unexpectedly, Wes put his arm around her shoulders as a late afternoon sun broke through the clouds and created a myriad of jewels in the sparkling waterfall.

The heavenly beauty defied description and Caroline shivered just looking at it.

"Are you cold?" he asked as he turned her

around and held her in the warm circle of his embrace.

She was dismayed by the swell of emotion that flooded through her. Sharing this moment with him had created unexpected feelings she didn't understand. When his fingertips began to lightly trace the soft curve of her cheek, she willed him to stop but a stirring of unbidden feelings kept her motionless.

He lowered his mouth to hers and brushed her moist lips, gently at first, then he deepened the kiss until heat radiated throughout her whole body.

Frightened by her unbridled response to his kisses, she pulled away and searched his face. He was smiling at her in a way that made her think he'd expected this to happen.

Part of the tourist package offered by Shadow Mountain Lodge.

She pushed away from him and headed in the direction of the tethered horses. Indignation came to her rescue as she fought to regain her emotional balance. Undoubtedly, Wes Wainwright had brought many female companions to this very spot and would probably bring many more. Maybe kisses, caresses and promises of hot passion were always included.

She took off the white hat and flung it into the bushes. How often had he planted kisses on willing lips shaded by that brim?

"What's going on?" he demanded as he caught up with her.

"That's exactly what I was wondering."

"I don't get it," he said. "If I didn't know better I'd think you were pretending to be sweet sixteen and never been kissed."

She ignored the sarcasm. Undoubtedly he was used to feminine invitations and ploys that invited his amorous attention and he probably stayed clear of women who weren't pleasant, accommodating companions. Obviously, his masculine pride was smarting over the whole incident.

"I'm chilled to the bone," she answered in a kind of double entendre.

He was silent for a moment and then said curtly, "I'll get you a saddle blanket."

On the ride back to the lodge, their previous, easy companionship was gone. Caroline was grateful for Wes's stony silence. She'd made enough of a fool of herself for one day.

By the time they reached the stables, the last rays of a setting sun had disappeared and shadows were deepening on wooded slopes of craggy high mountains.

They left the horses in the hands of the stablemen and when they entered the lodge through the front door, Caroline's thoughts were still on the afternoon ride that had gone wrong.

Felicia was just coming down the main staircase as they came in. She was alone and

Caroline suddenly realized she hadn't thought about Danny in any way during the outing. Hurriedly, Caroline crossed the room and met Felicia at the bottom of the stairs.

"Where's Danny?"

Felicia stiffened and her dark eyes flashed. "The children came down to get more books. I was delayed slightly and they went ahead. They're waiting in the reading room. They ran out of things to do. Neither of them would settle down for a nap."

"I'm sorry," Caroline said quickly. "I'll have a talk with Danny."

"And I'll speak to Cassie," Wes promised.

Felicia frowned as if she didn't think talking would do a lot of good.

"I really appreciate your looking after him." Caroline said. A strained weariness was evident in the nanny's voice.

"The two of them play off the other. What one doesn't think up, the other one does."

Sighing, she added, "They're precious children—but a handful."

"We'll look after them until bedtime," Wes said with obvious irritation.

Caroline was anxious to get Danny and escape from Wes's glowering presence.

The door to the reading room was open, but there was no sign of the children. No books lay on the floor. No chairs were out of place. Nothing indicated two youngsters had even been there.

"I told them to stay here until I came after them," Felicia said in an exasperated tone. "Now, where have they run off to?"

"Don't worry, we'll find them," Wes promised with a stern edge to his voice. "Go back to your rooms, Felicia. Maybe they went upstairs the back way and you missed them."

Mumbling to herself, she nodded and hurried out of the room.

"Let's check the social room," Wes said. "The kids probably got sidetracked, especially if there's any food or drink set out. Cassie's been known to help herself when she finds a snack anywhere around." He didn't seem worried, just irritated.

Caroline tried to ignore an unfounded tightness in her chest. She'd never thought of herself as an overanxious mother, but Danny had never been in strange surroundings like these before. And neither had she!

She kept pace with Wes's long stride and listened for echoing laughter or high-pitched voices as they approached the room. When they went in they found it as silent and empty as the hall had been.

Where could they have gone?

Wes frowned as if he was asking himself the same question. "Maybe they decided to go to my suite and get some books, instead of the reading room. Cassie has a boxful in my front closet."

"You're probably right," Caroline agreed

with instant relief. She'd seen all the stuff the little girl had pulled out. "They wouldn't even think about Felicia looking for them in a different place."

Quickly mounting the stairs to the second floor, they hurried down the long hall to Wes's suite.

"Cassie," he called as they went in.

No answer. The living room echoed with emptiness. A lack of clutter told them it wasn't likely that two wayward six-year-olds had been there.

Wes checked the bedrooms and bathroom. "They haven't been here."

"Maybe our rooms. Danny might have wanted to show Cassie the animal heads and they could have easily been distracted from going downstairs."

The hope died when they found her rooms as empty as Wes's suite.

"Okay, we'll go back downstairs and check the kitchen," Wes said impatiently. "Maybe they decided to hit Trudie up for a treat before getting the books. Cassie knows there's always something for her sweet tooth."

Caroline could tell Wes was still just irritated, not worried, and she tried to control her own uneasiness. After all, six-year-olds couldn't be expected to stick to any one plan for very long—especially if cookies or candy were in the offering.

Hank was busily tending to a roast that had just come out of the oven when they checked the kitchen. He shook his head when Wes asked if he'd seen Cassie and Danny.

"Nope. They didn't come in here. Better ask Trudie. She's been busy setting up the dinner buffet. They might have been pestering her. I thought Felicia was watching them?"

"They got away from her," Wes said.

Chuckling, Hank said, "I'd rather keep track of a couple of wild squirrels than those two."

When they asked Trudie if she'd seen them,

she said, "Nope, haven't seen hide nor hair of them. And I spent the afternoon doing some spot cleaning both upstairs and down." She frowned. "Maybe you ought to ask Tim and Dexter. They've been in the game room most of the afternoon. The kids could have been watching them play pool."

Wes's growing impatience showed when they entered the game room and found Dexter sitting alone in one of the leather chairs drinking a can of beer. Signs of a recent pool game were on the table.

"Want to play a couple of games, Wes?" Dexter asked eagerly as they came in. "I'm all warmed up, buddy. Beat Tim three games in a row," he bragged.

"We're looking for Cassie and Danny," Wes answered shortly. "Have they been in here?"

"Nope. Haven't seen them all day. I thought they were upstairs with Felicia while you two were taking your romantic ride to the falls."

Caroline stiffened at his reference to a romantic ride and resented the smirk that accompanied it.

"The kids were supposed to be in the reading room," Wes said curtly. For the first time his manner radiated a growing concern that had not been there before.

"Tim might have seen them," Dexter offered with a shrug as if he didn't understand what all the rush was about tracking them down. "I think he's in his office."

Caroline wonder if it was anger or anxiety that pulled at the corner of Wes's mouth. "If they come in you keep tabs on them," he ordered.

He swung on his heel and Caroline had trouble keeping pace with him as he led the way toward the back of the house. She kept telling herself the children were safe somewhere in the lodge.

They had to be!

Tim wasn't in his office but Shane was unpacking some boxes in an adjoining storeroom. "If you're looking for my mom, she took off with Tim somewhere." His tone was full of resentment. "I didn't ask where."

"Have you seen Cassie and Danny anywhere around?"

"Not for an hour or so. They were playing some kind of stupid game. They asked me if I wanted to play," he added in a disgusted tone.

"What kind of game?"

He shrugged. "They were following some kind of a treasure map."

"Did you get a look at the map?" Caroline demanded before Wes could.

"Nope. But I think Cassie said something about hiking up to the hunting cabin—"

"And you didn't stop them!" Wes exploded. The fury in his eyes made Shane take a step backward. "What in the hell were you thinking?"

"I'm not their babysitter," he snapped.

"Damn it, Shane!" Wes swore as he put his

face just inches from his nephew's. "If anything happens to them, you'll answer to me! That's a rough climb for anyone in the middle of the day, let alone two kids when it's almost dark. There are a hundred places to miss your footing and fall." He swung around to Caroline. "You stay here and I'll go after them."

"Where is the cabin?" she demanded in a strained voice, staying at his heels as he left the lodge by the back door.

"At the top of the ridge."

Wes headed for a rugged path behind the lodge that led upward through a heavy drift of evergreen trees. He knew Caroline would have trouble keeping up with him. The climb was not an easy one and even though the path was fairly well defined, it rose steadily upward.

The lodge's two-room cabin had been built for use during the hunting season and could only be reached on foot because the terrain was not suitable for horseback riding.

Even in bright sunlight the footing was precarious and this late in the day shadows had begun to spread over the rugged terrain making the ground deceptive in places where the path narrowed, or dipped dangerously with loose rocks. Only a couple of hours of fading daylight remained.

Wes tried to remember how many times he'd taken Cassie up the mountainside with him. Not many. He'd held her hand all the way every time, making sure to steady her footing when the climb became arduous and dangerous.

Nervous sweat beaded his brow as he imagined what could happen to two unwary six-year-olds on such treacherous slopes and high precipices. If they slipped and fell—

He jerked his thoughts away from a horror that sent an icy chill down his spine. What in the hell was all this about a treasure map? Shane had said they were playing some kind of game.

Cassie was certainly capable of creating some childish fantasy and Danny would go along with it if only to prove he was as brave as any girl. If they got off the path, no telling where they would end up. They could easily get lost amongst the trees and fallen rocks.

He repeatedly called out their names as they climbed upward. "Cassie! Cassie! Danny!" They both held their breath as they strained to hear any responding cry.

Nothing!

The only sound was the rustling of wild birds in the high treetops. Wes knew that night predators would be on the prowl as soon as darkness claimed the mountainside.

He bounded upward at increasing speed until he heard Caroline's frightened gasp. He swung around.

She'd fallen and was sliding dangerously backward on a narrow ledge. Racing back down the path, he grabbed her and carefully helped her back to her feet. "Easy does it."

"I'm all right," she said, wiping the dirt from her cheek.

Even though he admired her stubbornness, he wanted to lash out at her for not staying at the lodge. As they labored up the steep mountainside, the path ahead was even steeper and darker where thick stands of pine and spruce trees hugged the rocky rim.

Wes knew they had to make it to the cabin before darkness settled in on the mountain. They'd never find it safely in the dark. Even now the gray light of a fading day was claiming its hold on Shadow Mountain.

"We're almost there," he assured her finally as they climbed the last steep incline. "The cabin is just ahead."

The words were barely out of his mouth when a whiff of smoke touched his nostrils.

"What the—"

As the cabin came into view, he could see a trail of black smoke rising against the evening sky.

Chapter Seven

"Fire!" Wes plunged forward at a dead run over the rough ground. His breath was short at this high altitude and his hands and face were scratched by needled branches as he thrust them aside.

The pungent smell of burning wood was stronger as he ran toward the cabin but he couldn't see any flames. As he came closer, he realized the smoke was spiraling up from the chimney.

Relief was short-lived.

The fear that the children had never made it as far as the cabin was still with him as he reached the planked door and threw it open. The scene that met his eyes was so unexpected that for a long moment he just froze in the doorway.

Cassie and Danny were sitting on the floor in front of the fireplace sharing an open bag of potato chips.

"Whatcha doing here, Daddy?" Cassie greeted him with total innocence.

Danny went on munching the potato chips without showing any concern that an adult had showed up.

Wes swallowed hard. He'd never been so relieved—and so angry. When he heard Caroline's running footsteps, he turned around quickly.

"They're all right," he assured her as he stepped aside and let her enter.

"Danny," she gasped. "Thank God!" She threw herself down beside him and taking him in her arms, kissed him, stroked his hair and anxiously searched his face.

"Why is she crying?" Cassie asked, looking up at her father with innocent puzzlement.

"Because she was worried about him!"

"Were you worried about me, too, Daddy?"

"Damn right I was worried," he snapped.

"Then why aren't *you* crying?" she asked.

He took a deep breath as he eased down beside her. As he gave her a hug, he closed his eyes and let relief pour through every cell in his body. Then he said, "Honey, I'm not crying but I was scared, too. You must never do something like this again."

"Okay."

"I mean it. Don't you ever leave the lodge without my permission. Understand?"

"Don't be mad, Daddy. I wanted to tell you but you were gone." Cassie's petulant tone somehow put the blame on him.

"You both should have known better," Caroline said, looking Danny straight in the eyes.

"Nobody said we couldn't go," he argued.

"Did you ask anyone?" she countered sternly.

"Cassie knew the way. And the door was open," he added as if that made everything all right.

"Who lit the fire?" Wes asked. The last occupant of the cabin always left one log laid in the fireplace and there was a box of wooden matches on the mantel.

"I did." Cassie smiled proudly. "Felicia showed me how. She let me light one for her lots of times. First, you strike a match. Then quickly drop it in the middle on the paper and wood." Her eyes sparkled. "And then you have a fire."

"All right, but you know better than to play with matches," he lectured as he picked up the match box lying on the floor beside her.

"We were cold," Danny piped up.

"And it was getting dark," Cassie added, giving Danny a grateful look for his support.

"We couldn't find anything to eat 'cept these

potato chips," Danny complained, getting into the flow of defending themselves.

"Well, you're safe. That's the important thing," Caroline said with a deep sigh of relief as she put an arm around her son and held him close.

Wes glanced out the window at the darkening landscape. Night was falling fast. Trying to return to the lodge could be a disaster. They'd have to spend the night here. When he'd arranged for the cabin to be made ready with provisions—bottled water, bedding and firewood for the approaching elk season—he'd never dreamed they'd be needed in such weird circumstances. As he glanced at Caroline, he felt uncomfortable in her presence. She was barely speaking to him. Somehow he'd completely misread the situation at the falls. He'd felt a strange harmony between them as they stood mesmerized by the power and beauty displayed before them.

When she'd looked at him with those deep, liquid blue eyes, her supple body had seemed to welcome his embrace and as his fingertips had traced the smoothness of her face and trembling lips, he couldn't help himself. An overwhelming urge to claim that sweet mouth had surged through him. He'd pulled her close and kissed her as an explosive sexual desire surged through him.

Then it had happened—total rejection! Her whole body had suddenly gone rigid and she'd forcibly shoved him away. Too late, he realized she was in a different space altogether. His romantic advances were totally unwanted. If they hadn't been swept up in this terrifying ordeal with the children, they probably could have successfully ignored each other and gone their separate ways.

In spite of her dishevelled appearance, she seemed totally relaxed now that Danny and Cassie had been found safe and sound. Thank heavens, she wasn't weeping and wailing and scolding her son and threatening punishment.

He certainly didn't need a hysterical female on his hands.

As she sat in front of the fire, her lovely face glowing with relief, he promised himself that he'd make it clear to her that he wasn't the least bit interested in any unwanted romantic intimacy. Maybe he'd been around a different kind of woman too long. He couldn't think of one of his acquaintances who would have reacted the way she had. In fact, he was slightly indignant that Caroline Fairchild had made such an issue of a few harmless kisses.

Going into the kitchen end of the room, he opened a cupboard and took down a kerosene lantern from a high shelf. The lighted lamp created a warm glow as he placed it on a small table in the center of the room near a long sofa covered by an Indian blanket. An assortment of scattered chairs included an old-fashioned rocker that matched with those in some old-time photographs hanging on the wall. Hikers and hunters who used the cabin weren't particular about the furnishings. An oak door beyond the fireplace opened into a second room which had a full-sized bed and a couple of cots.

"All right, kids," he said as he sat down again on the floor in front of the fire. "I want to know where you got the idea to come up here all by yourselves."

"It was Danny's idea," Cassie said quickly.

"Was not!"

"Was too!"

"That's enough." His stern gaze made both children squirm as he held up a hand to stop the volley of accusations. "What's this about a treasure map?"

Neither child answered. Their little mouths were clamped shut and their eyes rounded with apprehension. Obviously, they knew they were in deep trouble.

"It's all right," Caroline coaxed. "Show us the treasure map. Do you still have it?"

Slowly, Cassie stuck a hand in her jeans pocket, drew out a piece of rumpled paper and handed it to her father.

"I'll be damned," Wes swore.

Caroline moved closer to him. "Let me see."

In silence, they both studied it. The map was a very simple drawing. A rectangle with a roof was marked Lodge and the surrounding mountains were drawn as single arching lines. A line of arrows pointed the way from the Lodge along a path that zig-zagged upward to another simple drawing labeled Cabin with another arrow marked Treasure pointing to the door.

Wes's frown was a mixture of rage and disbelief. "What do you think of that?"

"It's amazingly easy to follow."

"Who drew it for you, Cassie?" Wes's tone warned his daughter he wanted a straight answer.

The little girl swallowed hard as if she were trying to think of an answer that would please him. Caroline reached out and squeezed the little girl's hand. "It's all right, honey. You can tell us. Who made the map?"

"I…I don't know," she finally stammered.

"I don't either," Danny echoed quickly.

"Where'd you get it, Cassie?" Wes asked as he tried for a softer tone. He knew he could be demanding and short-tempered when something frustrated him. It had never been easy for him to rein in his impatience. "Who gave it to you?"

"Nobody," Danny answered before Cassie could. "We found it. By her telephone. Didn't we, Cassie?"

She nodded.

"Are you making this up, Danny?" Caroline searched her son's face. "Cassie really has a telephone?"

"Not a real one," Wes explained quickly. "She has a little table with a pretend phone in the downstairs telephone alcove. She plays there sometimes when Felicia is busy making calls. Is that where you found the treasure map, Cassie?"

"Uh-huh. I wanted to show Danny the phone," she replied defensively as if she shouldn't have been anywhere near the alcove without an adult. "And there it was. Right on my desk."

"We were going to get books," Danny added, looking at his mother for approval.

"But you never went to the reading room, did you?" Wes said. Now he knew why. They'd stopped at the telephone and found the map.

Had someone deliberately left the map there for the kids to find?

Wes looked at Caroline and saw the same question in her eyes.

"Felicia has been making up games for them," Caroline told him.

He was surprised by the noticeable edge to her voice and hard speculative glint in her eyes. Surely, she didn't suspect Felicia of doing something so irresponsible? "She'd never do something like this," Wes replied flatly.

"Are you sure? Do you completely trust her?"

Her question made Wes wonder if Felicia had been talking to Caroline about the kidnapping. He knew the tragedy had rested heavily on Felicia's conscience all these years even though he'd done everything he could to show her that he trusted her completely with his remaining child. He'd always felt that her concern for Cassie that night by taking the baby into her own bed had saved his daughter from being kidnapped, too.

"Felicia would never put Cassie in jeopardy," he said firmly. "Nor Danny."

"She put the idea of hunting for treasure in their heads," Caroline insisted. "I know Felicia made up a game that sent them hunting for clues. They were running all over the place. This treasure map could be just another one of her ideas."

"She'd never send them on some dangerous hike like this one."

"Somebody did!" Caroline flared angrily.

"Yes, and I'll find out who," he promised. "At the moment, I'm inclined to think this is some of Shane's doing. Tim tries to keep a handle on him, but it's not easy. I think he has too much time on his hands. No doubt, he'd think it was a big joke to do something like this."

"He told us to save him some of the money," Cassie volunteered.

"But we're not going to give him any, are we, Cassie?" Danny said, giggling.

Wes just shook his head as he got to his feet. How could anyone talk sense into a couple of six-year-olds? "Come on, Caroline, I'll show you the rest of the cabin and we'll decide how to arrange things for spending the night."

At first, he thought she was going to refuse his extended hand to help her to her feet. She seemed hesitant about having any physical contact with him as she gave him her hand.

Her behavior irritated him. Out of some

nebulous need to prove his masculine superiority, he held her hand slightly longer than necessary. Very slowly he let his fingers slide away from hers. As a flush rose in her cheeks, he wondered if it was caused by anger or something else she wouldn't admit to herself.

Maybe I'll have to find out.

As CAROLINE followed him into the other small room, she knew her limited experience with powerful men was pitifully inadequate to deal with Wes Wainwright. She suspected he'd used the cabin for more than one rendezvous with a lady of his choice.

Motioning around the small bedroom, he said, "As you can see, there's a full-sized bed and two cots. We always leave extra bedding in that large chest and a couple of bedrolls." His expression was innocent enough, but she had the impression that he was deliberately trying to embarrass her when he added, "There's a small bathroom. It's designed like those at isolated highway rest stops, so I'm afraid privacy is rather limited."

"I've been camping and was raised on a primitive farm," she briskly informed him. "I think the children and I can manage." Then she asked sweetly, "And where will you be sleeping?"

To her surprise, he chuckled. "You're something else, my dear Caroline."

"I don't know what you mean."

"Probably not, and that's what makes you such a challenge."

Before she could summon a cool reply, Danny and Cassie bounded into the room shouting in unison, "We're hungry."

"Okay. Okay." Wes quickly held up a hand to stop the chant. "Now, which one of you wants to be the cook?"

"Not me!" Cassie giggled.

"We don't know how to cook," Danny said solemnly as if Wes was dumb not to know it.

"Oh, that's too bad." Wes shook his head sadly. "I guess we don't eat."

"My mother cooks good," Danny volunteered quickly.

"She does?" Wes acted surprised. "Well, now, do you think she could fix supper for us?"

Danny looked up at her. "Could you, Mom?"

"I could try," she answered solemnly. "First, we'll need to get a fire going in that old stove."

"I think I could handle that," Wes replied

"I could show you how," she offered, unable to resist the temptation to tease him. After all, she was sure the task wasn't one listed in his portfolio.

"I bet you could." He chuckled. "Well, come on. Let's see what we can scare up to feed these hungry yahoos."

Wes built the fire while Caroline opened cans of baked beans, Vienna sausages and mixed fruit. The children filled their paper plates and sat cross-legged in front of the fire to eat.

Wes and Caroline sat at a small fold-down table in the kitchen area. Trying to keep the conversation on a nonemotional level she asked questions about the cabin. "Does it get a lot of use?"

"Usually just overnight. During elk season, mostly."

"You enjoy hunting then?"

"Your tone reveals where you stand on the matter."

"Yes, I guess it does," she admitted. "All those animal trophies at the lodge turn my stomach. I think it's a horrible sport."

"Sometimes hunting is not a sport but a necessity."

"Not in this day and age."

"That's where you're wrong," he said, leaning back in his chair. "Once this land belonged to the Indians. They lived off of it until the U.S. government moved them south onto dry, barren land. No more fresh venison or buffalo meat to feed their families." He looked grim. "We stole their livelihood from them. When I kill deer every year, it's not just for sport. We load up a freezer van and deliver the meat to Indian reservations in New Mexico."

She was embarrassed by her totally wrong assumption that he killed only for sport. "I'm sorry, I guess I jumped to the wrong conclusion."

His eyes took on a hard glint that startled her. "On the other hand, I'm sure I could kill someone who threatened my life or the welfare of my family."

She suddenly felt a chill that had nothing to do with the cold drafts seeping into the cabin. His pleasing outward persona was girded by an iron will that only the foolish would challenge. When he spoke of shooting someone who threatened his family, she wondered if he was thinking of the kidnapper who had robbed him of his son.

If things had been less tense between them

she might have encouraged him to talk about the hideous crime. She certainly could sympathize with the heartbreak he'd endured.

As soon as Danny and Cassie had finished eating, they began to quarrel. Tired and fussy, they wouldn't do anything without an argument and bedtime was something of a challenge.

Wes made ready to sleep on the couch while Caroline settled Danny and Cassie on the cots.

At the last minute, she gave in to Danny's pleas to let him sleep in the big bed with her.

"That's not fair," the little girl protested with pouting lips.

"Is too," Danny argued. "She's my mom."

Caroline quickly intervened. "You can sleep in the big bed, too, Cassie. There's room for three of us. We'll all be warmer in the same bed, anyway."

She had just snuggled the little girl in on one side and Danny on the other when Wes appeared in the doorway. When he saw the three of them in bed together, he teased, "Isn't there room for me, too?"

"No, Daddy," Cassie answered sleepily. "You can use a cot."

"Thanks, but I think I'll stay with the couch," he said. "Sleep tight—"

"—And don't let the bedbugs bite," Cassie and Danny piped up in unison.

Laughing, he went into the other room, leaving the door ajar.

The children fell asleep almost immediately, but Caroline lay wide awake, staring at the rough pine ceiling. Emotional tension created by her fear for their safety lingered. Her muscles ached from the arduous climb and she couldn't get comfortable sandwiched between the children. Finally, she gave up and decided she'd move to one of the cots.

As she slipped out of bed she saw the flicker of light from the lamp coming through the half-open bedroom door. She had discarded her jeans and jacket and remained in her blouse and underwear for sleeping. Taking one of the blankets from a cot, she wrapped it around herself and boldly walked out into the living-room area.

Wes was sitting on the floor with his arms wrapped around his pulled-up legs as he stared at the fire. He looked up at her with a questioning frown.

"Something the matter?"

"Can't sleep."

"Join the club."

"I think I will." She eased down on the rug beside him.

After several minutes of silence, he said, "What we both need is a good strong drink."

He went to a kitchen cupboard and came back with a bottle of brandy and two shot glasses.

"Oh, I couldn't," she protested quickly.

Ignoring her, he poured out two drinks of equal amounts. "Hold this one," he ordered. "You don't have to drink it."

"Then why do I have to hold it?"

"So it can talk to you." He eased down beside her. "And if you don't drink it, I will."

She smiled. "Fair enough."

He resumed his former relaxed position on the floor and seemed content to ignore her as they gazed at the fire. The wind had come up and they could hear branches scraping against the outside walls.

She was surprised when he said, "I'm sorry about what happened at the falls. The moment just felt special. Hard to explain."

She took a sip of brandy and her voice was husky as she admitted, "I think the mistake was mine. Somehow I thought the kiss was part of your usual package deal. You know, an exhilarating horseback ride, a beautiful water-fall and a come-on kiss."

"I've been at Cascade Falls more times than I can count…and never a kiss. I just felt the two of us were sharing something special." He shook his head as if he didn't know quite how to put it into words. "But when I kissed you, something changed."

"I guess that's why it scared me."

"Why?"

"I hadn't been kissed like that in a very long time," she admitted.

"That's a shame," he murmured as he gently turned her chin in his direction and brought his mouth tantalizingly close to hers.

A longing to feel his lips once again on hers challenged her pride. Was he manipulating her feelings again? She might have surrendered to the spiraling sexual attraction between them if the quiet of the night had not suddenly been shattered by raised voices in the bedroom.

"Move!"

"You're on my side of the bed."

"Am not."

"Are too!"

"Daddy!"

"Mommy."

Caroline sighed.

Wes grumbled. "What rotten timing."

Chapter Eight

Sometime in the middle of the night, Wes got up, threw some more wood on the fire and then stretched out on the couch again and dozed until about daybreak.

When he sat up, he listened for some sign that Caroline and the children were awake but there was no hint of movement in the bedroom. They'd probably sleep for another hour or two.

Going into the kitchen area, he built a fire in the stove and set a coffeepot on the back burner. He knew there was dry cereal in a metal canister and some canned milk. The kids would probably turn up their noses but they'd have to forgo pancakes and chocolate milk this morning. As soon as they had breakfast, they'd start back down the mountain. The trail would be easier to follow in the daylight.

As he glanced out the window his heart lurched.

It was beginning to snow!

"Damn!" he swore. A heavy Colorado storm could sock them in with high drifts. He turned on his boot heels and headed for the bedroom.

"Everybody up," he ordered as he came through the doorway. "We're leaving!"

Caroline's head came up from the pillow. "What's… what's the matter?" she stammered.

"It's beginning to snow! No telling how long it would take us to dig out if the storm settles in. We've got to make it down the trail before it gets covered."

She was on her feet in an instant and reaching for her jeans but the children didn't even move.

Wes pulled back the blankets covering them. "Okay, buckeroos. On your feet."

When the cold air hit them, Danny and Cassie curled up even tighter without opening their eyes. Weary from their strenuous climb, they weren't ready to get out of bed this early in the morning.

"Wake up! Wake up," he urged and gently jostled them. With determined effort, he finally got them out of bed. Then he made sure the kitchen was safely secure.

After what seemed like a frustrating eternity to him, the kids were finally dressed and he grabbed some small blankets to wrap around them.

He'd found a large man's woolen coat that had been left in the cabin and tossed it to Caroline. "Put this on."

"What about you?"

"My leather jacket will be enough. Let's go."

When he opened the front door a swirl of wind and snowflakes hit him in the face. The air was frigid, but he was relieved to see that only an inch of whiteness had collected on the ground so far. If they could keep ahead of any heavy snowfall the trail would be visible most of the way.

He grabbed Cassie's hand and took the lead with Caroline and Danny following. They had left the clearing and started downward through a thick stand of pine trees when Wes realized the snow was coming down at a faster rate than when he had looked out the kitchen window. As they bent their heads against the increasing wind and whipping snow, they moved forward at an excruciatingly slow pace.

The children held them back. Several times they would have tripped and fallen if they hadn't been holding on to an adult's hand. Clutching their blankets, they were slow-moving, their steps uncertain on the rough ground.

Cassie whimpered when the flakes began to coat her face. Wes could hear Caroline trying to reassure Danny. He knew he could carry one of them but not both. Maybe he'd made a mistake, thinking they could make it down to the lodge before the storm really hit. Turning back now would mean they'd have to climb back up the steep incline and lose the progress they'd already made down the path.

As the minutes passed, the nightmare grew. Snow began to change trees, rocks and ground into an unfamiliar white terrain. The path began to disappear. The wind began to paralyze them with its biting cold.

Their steps were shorter and slower and Wes thought he was hallucinating when he glimpsed a movement on the trail below. Slowly, a figure came through the falling snow and Wes couldn't believe it when someone held up a hand and waved.

Tim Henderson!

Wes had never been so glad to see the big-boned, soft-spoken Texan. He couldn't find the words to show his relief that help had arrived.

"We were pretty worried about you all," Tim

told him. "When you didn't come back from the cabin by nightfall we decided you'd found the kids. Then, this morning, with the snow starting, I decided to check."

"Thank God you did."

"With the trail drifted over, you'd have to wait until the snowdrifts cleared."

"It's been rough going. The kids can't hack it. We'll have to carry them."

Tim nodded.

"You take the boy." Wes turned to Caroline. "I'll carry Cassie. You stay between me and Tim."

She nodded and he turned away quickly before he gave in to an absurd impulse to hold her close and brush the snowflakes from her eyelashes. As they started down the snow-covered trail again, he silently vowed to make someone pay for putting her through this hell.

Under normal circumstances, when the rough ground and shelves of rocks were clearly visible, the mountain trail was challenging enough. Now, in the growing storm needled boughs of overhanging trees sagged with the weight of collecting snow.

Every minute seemed like an eternity to Caroline. In the whipping wind and falling snow every rocky ledge or pile of boulders seemed like all the others. She just kept putting one foot in front of the other, matching her footsteps with the imprints of Tim's large boots. She had no idea how far below the lodge nestled against the rugged mountain slope.

With every treacherous step, she was relieved that Danny was safe in Tim's strong arms as the man kept a steady, knowing pace ahead of her.

When the roof of the lodge became visible below through the snow-laden trees she heard Wes's chilled cry, "We made it!"

Relief caught in her own throat. She felt like

shouting when Danny peered over Tim's shoulder and gave her a weak smile. He was safe. That was all that mattered.

They entered the lodge through the back door to Tim's office. No sign of a welcoming committee. The morning silence was undisturbed. Apparently, Tim was the only one who had risen at dawn to hunt for them.

As the men set the shivering children down, Wes said, "We need to get them into a warm bath and some dry clothes." Caroline covered her blue lips with her hands and blew on them before she stroked Danny's chilled face. "It's okay, honey. It's okay."

Wes took Cassie's hand. "Tim, alert Hank and Trudie to get a hot breakfast ready for us." Then he nodded at Caroline. "We'll take the back stairs."

Wes and Cassie led the way up the servants' stairway to the second floor.

When they came through a door that opened

into the hall, they heard a loud high-pitched cry and jerking their heads in that direction they saw Felicia running down the hall toward them. The nanny was still in her nightclothes, her hair loose and flying like gray-black wings on her shoulders.

"I saw you coming from my window," she gasped when she reached them. "All night I kept candles and incense burning. Oh, my poor baby, my poor baby," she sobbed as she embraced Cassie. "Are you all right?"

"I'm hungry."

Felicia's hysterics were in sharp contrast to Cassie's flat reply and Caroline thought Wes's lips seemed to curve in a secret smile at his daughter's matter-of-fact response.

"She's fine, Felicia. Bring her down to breakfast after she has a warm bath and dry clothes." He nodded at Caroline. "Let's do the same."

When they reached her bedroom door, he opened it for her and Danny. She was about to follow her son inside when Wes put a detaining hand on her arm.

She searched his thoughtful expression. "What is it?"

"I just wanted you to know that if I had a choice of getting snowbound with anyone, it would be with you. I know you don't believe me but it's true. I've never met another woman who could have handled the situation with such courage."

He turned away before she had a chance to reply and disappeared down his end of the hall.

Later when she and Danny went downstairs for breakfast, she was still mulling over the surprising compliment. She knew there were too many hidden levels to Wesley Wainwright to take him at face value. At the moment, it seemed enough that a positive, fragile relationship might be in the making.

Even before she and Danny reached the dining room, she could hear raised voices.

Pausing a moment in the doorway, she saw Wes and Stella standing at one end of the buffet, facing each other.

Stella was holding a full plate but Wes's hands were empty and clutched at his side. Their expressions verified that they were in a heated argument.

Caroline quickly led Danny to a table. She didn't want to be drawn into their confrontation by joining them at the buffet.

"I tell you, Shane didn't have anything to do with it," Stella insisted in a strident voice. "I can't believe you'd suggest such a thing."

"And I can't believe he didn't stop the kids," Wes retorted angrily. "He knows how dangerous that trail is. And he knew they were going to the cabin. They showed him the map."

"All right, I agree that he should have told someone what they were up to but he's a teenager living in his own world. Give him some slack."

"Someone deliberately drew that map," Wes countered.

"And you've already decided that it was Shane. Well, I have news for you. This whole situation reeks of your hunting buddy's brand of humor...and jealousy."

"What are you talking about?"

"In case you haven't noticed, you've been spending more time with Caroline and the two kids than you have with Dexter. Why don't you ask him about this whole fiasco?"

Stella set her plate back on the buffet and with her head held high and her back rigid she walked out of the room. She must have passed Dexter in the hall because he came in just seconds later.

Giving a pretend shiver, he walked over to Wes. "Brr, it's as cold inside as it is outside. What's up with Stella? Jealousy?"

"Don't be stupid, Dex," Wes replied shortly.

Dex just grinned. "Tim tells me you spent a

cozy night in the cabin with our lovely decorating lady. How did you arrange that?"

Wes said something to Dexter that Caroline couldn't hear but Dexter's smile instantly disappeared.

"Wait a minute, Wes. I didn't know until this morning that you guys were even gone."

"Are you sure, Dex?" Wes asked. His eyes narrowed as he studied his friend.

"Damn sure! If you want to know, I drank my dinner last night. You know how I am sometimes. Too much Scotch and I have to sleep it off. Why don't you tell me what's going on?" His eyes slid knowingly to where Caroline was sitting. "I can't say that I blame you for using the cabin for more interesting things than a hunting party."

Heat surged up in Caroline's cheeks. She shoved back her chair. "Stay here, Danny. I'll get our breakfast."

Wes maneuvered Dexter over to one of the

other tables. "Meet me in my suite after break-fast, Dex," he said abruptly and then walked back to Danny and sat down at the table beside him.

Caroline quickly filled two plates and was relieved when Dexter completely ignored her. He stayed at his table, drinking black coffee. No doubt about it, he looked like someone with a brute of a hangover.

Wes had already opened a carton of milk for Danny and poured two cups of coffee when Caroline returned to the table.

"Aren't you eating?" she asked as she sat down opposite him.

"I had something in the kitchen earlier. I wanted to quiz Trudie and Hank. They know pretty much what's going on most of the time."

"And—?"

He shook his head. "Hank said Tim made some telephone calls on the hall phone yesterday afternoon but Trudie didn't see anyone near Cassie's desk when she dusted earlier in the day."

"Do you think someone put the map there knowing that sooner or later Cassie would find it?"

"I believe Hank and Trudie when they say they didn't see it there," Wes answered. "Tim said he didn't know anything about the map. He heard about it from Shane last night."

Caroline frowned. "Have you talked to Shane?"

"No, I decided to talk with his mother first. You saw how that went over. Stella's always been too protective of Shane for his own good."

"Mothers are often like that," Caroline admitted as she glanced at Danny. Even though he was busily licking grape jelly off his toast, she knew her son was taking in the conversation at some level. More than once Danny had repeated with embarrassing results something he'd overheard. She certainly didn't want Wes to launch into any tirade about Stella's parenting skills that might be repeated. Working professionally with the woman was difficult enough without battling any emotional issues.

"Where's Cassie?" Danny piped up, his lips and fingers sticky with jelly.

"Having breakfast upstairs with Felicia as usual." Wes nodded at Caroline. "You can leave Danny whenever you're ready."

She answered as evenly as she could, "After what's happened, I may keep a short leash on him myself."

"Why is that?"

Wes's obvious trust and confidence in the woman puzzled Caroline. Surely, he must feel that the woman was responsible for a situation that had left his infant son vulnerable to kidnappers?

"She's the logical one to have drawn the map," Caroline replied evenly. "It fits in with the other games she created for the kids."

"You're not blaming Felicia for what happened, are you?"

"I don't know who to blame," she admitted. "Maybe Felicia made the map for some harmless activity. Someone else could have thought it would be a joke to place it by Cassie's telephone and see what the children did with it." Caroline sighed. "I don't know what happened, but Felicia was the one who was supposed to be looking after them."

"I agree she shouldn't have trusted them to go straight to the reading room, but she would never endanger their lives, I know that."

"Someone did."

"It couldn't have been intentional. Just bad judgment."

Caroline couldn't tell if he was trying to convince himself or her. There were deep creases in Wes's forehead when Dexter got up and left the room without looking in their direction.

"Have you known him a long time?" Caroline asked.

"I can't even remember when Dex wasn't

hanging around," Wes admitted. "He was best man at my wedding. When we were young, he had more money to spend than I did and Dex was generous to a fault. When we were in college, our family fortunes changed. My father made wise investments and extended our financial holdings beyond our cattle ranch. Dexter's family didn't fare so well. I've tried to be there for him when he needs a friend."

"You don't think he'd do something stupid like draw that treasure map?"

Wes's jaw visibly tightened. "Sometimes Dex's sense of humor gets out of bounds, I'll admit. His practical jokes have backfired more than once, but they've never presented any real danger to anyone."

"I don't like him," Danny said with childish solemnity.

Both Caroline and Wes were startled. "Why not?" Caroline asked quickly.

"He tickles."

"When does he do that?" She didn't know Dexter had been with Danny when she wasn't around.

"When he counts my ribs. And Cassie's, too. He says boys have one less rib than girls. Felicia tells him to get lost."

"I see," Caroline said, forcing a smile. "Well, I think I'll tell him the same thing."

Wes shoved back his chair and stood up. "I'll talk to him. Oh, I almost forgot. I promised Cassie that she and Danny could enjoy the Jacuzzi this afternoon. It'll warm them up." He paused. "You might want to join them, Caroline."

"Without a bathing suit?" she impulsively asked with mock solemnity.

"Especially without." His smile was an open challenge.

WES WORKED through the noon hour taking care of matters referred to him by his various executive teams. His original plans to shorten his time at the lodge had been pushed aside for reasons he still couldn't quite define. The arrival of Caroline Fairchild shouldn't have changed his intent to leave—but it had. Now, this latest near tragedy demanded that he stay and make certain nothing like it happened again.

Standing at the window, he was looking out at heavy drifts of snow piling up around the lodge when Cassie arrived with Felicia.

"I'm ready, Daddy," she said as she pranced in wearing a pink bathing suit, terry-cloth robe and rubber thongs. Felicia had braided her blond hair and fastened the ends with pretty seashell barrettes.

"Wow, aren't you pretty," he said, hugging her. "You look ready for an afternoon at the beach."

"Why aren't you ready?" Cassie scowled at his sweater and slacks.

"It's just you and Danny today," he told her. He knew Stella might have a couple of bathing suits, but he doubted Caroline would ever borrow one.

"Do you want me to come, too?" Felicia asked as if feeling insecure about letting Cassie out of her sight after what had happened.

"No, I'll bring her back to your apartment in about an hour."

She nodded and gave Cassie one last look as if reassuring herself that all was well. Her soft slippers and full skirt made a whispering sound as she left.

"All right, let's go, my little mermaid," he said taking her hand.

"Daddy, I have feet," she corrected him as if he didn't know anything at all.

"So you do. And pretty ones at that."

A misty warmth greeted them when they entered the small Jacuzzi room and an inviting gurgle of bubbling water filled their ears. The sunken Jacuzzi was recessed in a tiled floor and a couple of chairs and one reclining lounge were set nearby.

No sign of Danny or Caroline. Maybe she'd

changed her mind about coming, Wes thought and was startled by the wave of disappointment that went through him.

Cassie quickly kicked off her thongs and threw off her robe. Wes stood by as she carefully descended the stairs and began bobbing in the water and trying to splash him.

He wasn't aware that Danny and Caroline had come into the room until Cassie suddenly squealed, "Hurry up, Danny! Hurry up!"

"I'm coming." Danny called back. As the boy quickly discarded the bathrobe, Wes smiled to see that a pair of navy-blue underwear was serving as bathing trunks.

"Necessity is the mother of invention," Caroline told Wes with a chuckle.

"Too bad, you weren't just as inventive," he teased. "Maybe we ought to try this again later."

When she didn't follow through with a flirtatious response, he knew she wasn't used to engaging in sexual innuendoes. In some ways, her lack of sophistication was a pleasant change and in other ways it was totally frustrating. How could a man make time with a desirable female who refused—or didn't know how—to play the mating game?

Wes placed the two chairs close enough to the Jacuzzi to be ready for any sudden mishaps. He knew Cassie could be aggressive when she got caught up in any game.

As the two children were bouncing around, splashing each other like porpoises, he could tell Caroline was obviously on guard as she watched their water play.

"Do you like to swim?" Wes asked, fantasizing about those shapely legs and rounded breasts of hers in a bikini.

"I think I would," she answered with a slight frown. "Never had much of a chance to find out. Maybe I'll learn along with Danny."

"He likes the water all right. All boy, isn't he?" Wes said with an unexpected sense of envy.

A short time later, Caroline glanced at her watch. "I've put a load of clothes in the washer and dryer. Do you mind if I leave for a few minutes to tend to them?"

"Not at all. I'll keep everything under control. Don't worry, Danny will be safe," Wes assured her.

"Don't let him get too rough with Cassie."

Wes laughed. "Knowing my daughter, it will probably be the other way around."

She hurried out of the room heading toward the laundry room down the hall. He could tell that she was still reeling from the emotional trauma they'd all been through. Obviously she was apprehensive about letting her son out of her sight. Wes could understand her feelings. He still had reservations about trusting other people with Cassie.

He watched as the two youngsters splashed each other, squealing and laughing. Danny had lifted himself up on the edge of the Jacuzzi and, sitting there, he began furiously kicking the water, drenching Cassie in the spray.

Laughing and shoving back her sopping-wet hair she pointed to his feet. "You have funny toes. You have funny toes," she chanted.

"I do not."

"Do too! They're just like my daddy's."

Wes stared the boy's small toes curled in a funny twist back against the neighboring toe. He couldn't get his breath. Something exploded inside his head. He suddenly felt as if someone just dropped him off a thousand-foot cliff.

Chapter Nine

Caroline was in the laundry room longer than she had expected. When she took the clothes out of the dryer, she found a couple of pullovers still a little damp so she decided to give them another ten minutes while she folded the rest of the clothes.

She was just about finished when Stella walked by the door and then stopped when she saw Caroline. "Oh there you are," she said, coming into the laundry room. "Felicia said you were enjoying the Jacuzzi."

"Just the kids," Caroline said quickly. "Wes is watching them while I finish up the laundry."

"I wanted to apologize for this morning.

When Wes and I butt heads like that, I need some time to myself to cool down. I really didn't mean to ignore you."

"I understand," Caroline quickly assured her. "I wasn't in a very good mood myself."

"And for good reason! This whole thing is crazy. Why would anyone think up some dangerous game like that?" she asked and in the next breath she answered her own question. "Someone who knew the kids were into treasure hunts, that's who. I haven't seen the map, but I'm wondering if there's a clue as to who might have drawn it. You know, handwriting or kind of pencil or pen? I don't want Shane to bear the brunt of all this unfounded suspicion. It's not fair!"

Even though Caroline had to question whether Shane merited his mother's faith, she knew she'd feel the same way if it were her son involved. Still, she wanted to remind Stella that Shane was at fault for not stopping

Danny and Cassie when he knew about the map.

As Stella continued to blow off steam about Wes's unfair attitude toward her son, Caroline managed to hold her tongue.

"Shane always knocks himself out to please Wes. That's what makes all of this so unfair. I want to see that map. I'll know in a minute if Shane had anything to do with it."

"I'm sure Wes will gladly show it to you. We all want to find out who's responsible."

"I hope this unfortunate incident isn't going to affect moving ahead on our redecorating plans," she said bluntly. "I mean, even losing one day here and there can add up, you know."

Caroline knew then Stella was resentful that she'd accepted Wes's invitation for the kids to enjoy the Jacuzzi.

"Maybe we can put in a full day tomorrow, for a change?" Caroline responded sweetly.

Stella nodded. "I guess neither of us is in the

mood to look at paint charts and fabric swatches today."

"I'd like to get your decorating plans finalized as soon as possible," Caroline told her. More and more, she was feeling the necessity to complete her contract and have the security of some money in the bank. Then, go home.

As they parted in the hall, Stella headed in one direction and Caroline in the other. With her arms filled with folded clothes, Caroline hurried back to the Jacuzzi room.

Danny and Cassie were playing toss in the water with a large ball. She quickly apologized to Wes for being so long.

"Have they been behaving themselves?"

He stared at her for a long moment as if he hadn't even heard her question. Then he seemed to mentally shake himself. "Yes, fine."

"I had to wait for the dryer," she said, deciding not to mention her conversation with Stella.

He just nodded as he picked up the towels and

walked over to the steps. His expression displayed impatience as he said, "Time to get out."

Cassie shot her father a quick glance as if she knew from his tone not to argue. As she quickly dropped the ball, Danny grabbed it for one more throw.

Caroline couldn't tell whether Wes was going to reprimand Danny or let it pass, but the way his eyes narrowed on her son made her intervene. "Danny, let's go."

As they made their way back upstairs, Caroline was at a loss to know why Wes was no longer the relaxed, cordial host he'd been. She'd never seen him in this kind of mood.

For some reason he'd erected a wall between them. He seemed ready to explode about something. The hardness of his jaw and the way his hands were clenched frightened her.

When they reached her door, she quickly said, "Thank you. I know Danny enjoyed it."

"Me, too," Cassie said.

If the children hadn't been there, Caroline would have demanded an explanation. Obviously something had happened while she was in the laundry room—but what? He wasn't even like the same man. With a curt nod, he took Cassie's hand and walked away with his back and head as rigid as a board.

WES WAS ON THE PHONE to headquarters in Houston as soon as Felicia left his suite with Cassie. It was almost closing time but his secretary, Myrna Goodwin, was still in the office. She was a woman in her fifties who had also been his father's secretary.

When Myrna answered he said, "Good! I'm glad I caught you."

"Oh, hi, boss." Her tone was relaxed and friendly. "What's happening?"

"I need a telephone number. That private investigator who did that good job for us last year."

"Detective Delio?"

"That's the one." Wes waited with pen in hand.

After she'd checked she gave him two numbers. "One is his office and the other is his home. I don't suppose his cell phone will do you any good at the lodge."

"Give it to me. I may have to make a trip to Denver."

She knew from experience that he'd fill her in if and when it was necessary. She didn't ask why or try to find out what was on his mind.

He thanked her, hung up and fought an impulse to call Delio immediately. He knew that getting his emotions under control before making decisions and acting on them had served him well in the business world.

He'd never been faced with such a personal challenge as this one. The unusual curl of little toes had been a family aberration for several generations. Some blood relatives in the same family passed it on and some didn't. Wes had inherited the trait from his father but his brother, Delvin, and his son, Shane, had missed it.

Wes left his desk and began pacing the floor.

CAROLINE AND DANNY ate dinner early and she had just put him down for the night when she heard a knock on the sitting room door.

Who could that be?

Her frown changed to an expression of surprise when she saw Wes standing there.

"How about a nightcap? I decided we ought to end the day on a better note. What do you say?" He was smiling and holding two wine goblets and a bottle of chardonnay.

Her spirits lifted. His mood had made a hundred-and-eighty-degree turnaround. "I think I could handle that."

She realized how her feelings for him had moved into dangerous depths when his dis-arming smile sent a welcoming warmth through her. Somehow, she'd let this man touch her on emotional levels she'd jealousy guarded since Thomas's death. She'd never expected to feel that wonderful, compelling kind of euphoria again, but her heart had quickened just seeing him standing there, smiling at her.

"No ice but the wine is chilled," he assured her as he placed the glasses and bottle down on the small coffee table.

They sat down on the sofa, he poured the wine and handed her a goblet. Then he lifted his and toasted, "To the future."

"Whatever that may be," she agreed.

"The future is whatever we make it, isn't it?" he asked.

As his eyes met hers over the rim of his glass, she sensed his words had a double meaning, but she just sipped her wine and relaxed against the cushions beside him, grateful for his company.

He kept the conversation light and seemed

comfortable talking about the difficulties of raising a child and the challenges that went with parenting. She didn't know how the conversation led into a personal sharing of her past.

"Was your husband good with children?" he asked as he poured her a second glass of wine.

"Thomas was a good father and loved Danny deeply. Unfortunately, he didn't get to spoil him very much because he didn't have the time. His developing medical practice demanded a great deal." She sighed as she swirled the wine in her glass.

"That can happen," he agreed. "I've been there. Sometimes you have to have something shake you up before you realize what's important."

His fingers visibly tightened on his glass and she wondered if he was thinking about the loss of his son. "I don't know what I'd do if something happened to Danny."

"He's lucky to have a mother like you. I

expect you wanted more children," he said in a sympathetic tone.

The wine had loosened her tongue. "Yes, I wanted two boys and two girls, but it didn't happen." She felt at ease sharing her feelings with him. "I'll be forever grateful for Danny. I'd almost given up hoping."

"You had trouble getting pregnant?"

Her chest tightened with remembered pain as the past suddenly seemed as fresh as yesterday. Something in his voice brought all the disappointments flooding back. Her hand shook slightly as she set the empty wineglass down on the table without answering.

"I'm sorry," he quickly apologized, putting an arm around her shoulders and leaning his head close to hers. "If you don't you want to talk about it…?"

Strangely enough as she rested in the warm cradle of his arm, she realized how desperately she did want to talk about it. Maybe it was time to try and release all the pain and heartache of the past. She had kept it all bottled up much too long.

Taking a deep breath, she said, "I conceived two times. A boy and a girl."

"And you lost…the girl?"

"I lost them both."

He stiffened. "Both?"

She swallowed hard. "I couldn't carry either one of them to term. Some irreversible physical weakness causes me to miscarry." She finished her wine in two large gulps as hot tears spilled from her eyes and dribbled down her cheeks.

"But Danny?"

As if he heard his name, there was a movement inside the bedroom door and he appeared rubbing his eyes.

"Mommy?"

"What is it, honey?

"I'm thirsty. And you're making too much

noise," he whined as if someone had said those same words to him a few times.

"Let me get you a glass of water, Danny." Wes was instantly on his feet. "And I'll tuck you back in bed just the way I do Cassie, okay?" He took the little boy's hand in his and off they went to the bathroom.

Caroline leaned her head back against the sofa. Her head was swimming. How many glasses of wine had she had? Only two but she'd drunk them fast.

The alcohol had loosened her tongue. She couldn't believe she'd been divulging such personal things about herself. And to Wes Wainwright, of all people! She had no idea how the conversation had taken that direction. Her childlessness was not a subject for polite discussion, especially with a man she barely knew.

She could hear Danny's responding giggle as Wes tucked him in bed. His continuing attention to her and Danny surprised her.

When Wes came back into the sitting room and sat down closely beside her, he said, "He's a great boy. I envy you having a son like that."

"He's changed my life," she admitted. "And after Thomas passed away, I was doubly grateful we'd made the decision to take him. I love him as dearly as if he were my own flesh and blood."

"He's adopted?"

She nodded. "My husband knew I was devastated after my medical condition was determined to be irreversible. Thomas pushed for adoption. In fact, he arranged everything."

"Everything?" he echoed.

"Thomas didn't even tell me he'd located a baby boy until most of the legal work had been done."

"I see." Wes swirled the wine in his glass for a long moment and then set it down without taking a sip. "I guess being a doctor, he'd have access to adoptable babies."

"I never met the young unmarried woman

who gave the baby up," Caroline admitted. "Nor the lawyer who handled the adoption. I didn't want to know any of that." She firmed her chin. "From the moment Danny was put in my arms, I knew he was mine. All mine."

When Wes didn't respond, she looked up at him and instantly felt contrite. What a fool she'd been! The conversation must have brought back bitter memories of losing his only son under devastating circumstances.

"I'm sorry. I shouldn't have gone on like that. I didn't mean to bore you with all the episodes of my personal soap opera," she apologized quickly.

"No, I'm glad you did. Very glad. And I wasn't bored in the least. I'm grateful you were willing to share with me."

"So am I."

As she lifted her face to his, he gently brushed back a trailing curl on her cheek. His lips brushed her forehead with a light kiss.

Then, to her surprise, he drew back and firmly set her away from him.

She was at a loss how to lighten a situation that suddenly had become terribly uncomfortable.

His expression hinted at a guarded control as he rose to his feet. "I'd better let you get some rest. It's been a long day. Maybe I'll see you and Danny at breakfast?"

She nodded, not knowing if it was an invitation or a casual comment.

He paused at the door and looked back at her for a long moment as if he were tempted to come back and kiss her. Then he abruptly said, "Good night," and left.

After the door closed behind him and she heard his fading steps down the hall, she wondered why she felt more totally alone than she had before.

WES WENT straight to his desk and located Detective Delio's home telephone number. His hands were sweaty as he dialed the number. He knew it was late to be calling him, but he was filled with an urgency that defied common sense. It was as if six years of tortuous waiting had suddenly been swept aside. Danny was adopted.

He ignored an inner voice warning him that he could be inviting more heart-wrenching disappointment if what Caroline had said about the unmarried birth mother and the adoption was true. Still, she had admitted that her husband took care of everything. Maybe the good doctor had been less than honest. Wes knew he'd never rest until he was certain beyond any doubt that the boy's physical resemblance to his family was just happenstance.

When he had Delio on the line, Wes wasted no time with small talk. He'd worked with the small, energetic Italian before and they understood each other. In the past, Delio had been paid handsomely for getting several investigations done well and quickly. If the private investigator had been around six years ago when his son had been snatched from the nursery, Wes believed Delio might have uncovered some vital leads in the kidnapping.

"I need you to look into a Colorado adoption," Wes advised him in a crisp, businesslike tone.

"All right. I'll need some details."

"I don't know what agency handled it, but Thomas and Caroline Fairchild had a lawyer who was paid to take care of the legal process. I want you to come to Denver and scrutinize every detail of that adoption."

"What am I looking for?"

"Any evidence that the infant boy they adopted might be my son."

Delio gave a low whistle. "If I didn't know you better, Wes, I'd think you were guilty of wishful thinking."

"The boy has a physical trait like one inherent in my family line. What we need is some hard evidence and I'm willing to go to any lengths to get it. I have to follow through on this even though it seems like an impossibility in some ways."

"I understand."

"Good. Get on it right away."

"Sure thing."

"Call me here at the lodge as soon as you've checked out the adoption."

"Will do. And Wes, don't get your hopes up. This sounds like a real long shot."

"Maybe not," Wes countered briskly.

After he'd hung up the phone, he sat there for a long time staring at nothing. He'd had gut intuitions before, but never as strong as this one.

His thoughts raced ahead.

Caroline.

She'd touched him on an emotional level that he hadn't felt for a long time. He admired her independence, her courage and a feminine softness that she tried to hide. He was physically attracted to her. If things had been different… But they weren't!

He told himself that personal considerations had no place in correcting a terrible wrong like this one. He hated using Caroline's feelings in his efforts to find out the truth, but he had no choice. He had the right to claim his son and he couldn't let sentiment stand in the way. He vowed to do whatever was necessary to exert that right.

A peppering mixture of snow and ice hitting the windowpane was the only sound in the echoing rooms as he readied himself for the impending battle with Caroline over the young child who conceivably might be his son.

Chapter Ten

Caroline and Danny overslept the next morning. The snow storm had left behind a mantle of glittering white that was almost blinding in the bright sunlight.

"Let's get a move on, Danny," she said as she glanced at her watch. "Trudie will be clearing off the breakfast buffet."

They hurriedly dressed and were just about ready to leave when there was a knock on the bedroom door. They were surprised to see Cassie standing there.

"Felicia says to have breakfast with us. We've got cinnamon rolls with lots of frosting." Grinning at Danny, she rolled her eyes. "Yummy, yummy."

Danny perked up immediately and gave his mother a begging expression. "Can we?"

"Yes, of course. That's very nice of Felicia to invite us," Caroline said quickly, secretly relieved that she had an excuse not to face Wes this morning. She was totally embarrassed at the way she had dumped such an emotional load on him last night. Who could blame him for making a rather abrupt exit? Never had she talked so openly about her disappointing miscarriages—and to Wesley Wainwright of all people! She was mortified just thinking about it. He'd probably make a point of avoiding her from now on.

As that thought crossed her mind, the disappointment she suddenly felt surprised her. What had happened to her usual common sense? According to Dexter's gossip, Wes enjoyed having romantic affairs, but the fact that he'd never remarried made his intentions clear enough. A moment's pleasure was on his agenda.

Well, it's not on mine!

She resolved to put Wes Wainwright out of her mind and have the good judgment to see the situation as it really was. Her next challenge was pressuring Stella into finalizing the details for the redecorating project. The sooner, the better!

Much to Caroline's surprise and consternation, Felicia insisted on talking about Wes at breakfast. She waited until the children had eaten and were parked in the living room playing their car-racing game.

"Wes hides a heavy heart, I'm afraid," she said as she fixed her dark eyes on Caroline.

"Don't we all?" Caroline responded with a slight shrug. She wasn't in the mood to chat about a man who was dominating her thoughts too much already.

"You're very much like him."

Caroline lifted an eyebrow. "In what way?"

"Your heart needs mending, too. That's what the cards tell me."

"Maybe you ought to exchange them for a different deck," Caroline replied with a smile. "I assure you, Felicia, my heart is in a very good state and I intend to keep it that way. Your concern is misplaced."

"Your aura is not good." She seemed to be focusing on something above Caroline's head. "Very disturbed."

"Probably due to a lack of sleep," Caroline quipped.

Felicia sighed as she reached over and patted Caroline's hand. "I only want to prepare you."

"For what?" Caroline had never gone to a fortune teller or consulted a psychic and this kind of talk made her uncomfortable.

"I don't know. Something is not right. Like you, Wes hides his feelings. I'm afraid someone is going to get terribly hurt."

"I appreciate your concern, Felicia, but you

and your cards are way off base. As soon as I finish my commitment here, it's not likely there'll be any occasion that I'll see him again."

When Felicia fell silent, Caroline decided it was time to take her leave. "Thanks for breakfast. I'll collect Danny and get to work," she said as she rose from the table.

"You're not leaving him with me?"

"I think it's better if I keep a short rein on him."

"You think I made the treasure map." She fixed her accusing dark eyes on Caroline. "How can you think such a thing?"

"It's not that—" Caroline began.

"Protecting Cassie and her father is my life! Nothing else matters. I'd do anything for them. Anything. Don't you understand?"

"Yes," Caroline replied. Obviously, the poor woman was riddled with guilt because she'd failed to save Wes's infant son from the kidnappers. A chill went up Caroline's back as she wondered how twisted that devotion might be.

Danny put up a fuss about leaving, but Caroline was firm. Felicia had done nothing to reassure her Danny was in good hands under her care. In fact, her obsessive allegiance to Wes and Cassie sounded a warning. It wasn't Danny's welfare that would come first in any situation. Caroline decided she'd bring her son back to play with Cassie when she could stay with him.

Danny grumbled all the way to the workroom. Caroline knew she'd have to find a way to keep him busy and out of trouble while she moved ahead on the redecorating plans as quickly as possible.

She was surprised and delighted to find Stella in the workroom, waiting for her. The last time she'd seen her was in the laundry room while the children were with Wes in the Jacuzzi. Stella's bright smile was a relief.

"I've gone through these," she said, pointing to several open books. "And I have some ideas to run by you."

"Great," Caroline said. "We'd better line up some workmen to get started before winter really sets in."

"I've made some inquiries and found some reliable services in Telluride," Stella assured her. "We'll have to provide room and board for the workmen as we need them, but that's no problem. There are several rooms off the kitchen that are suitable for temporary occupancy."

A load of frustration rolled off Caroline's shoulders. Once the projected changes were approved, she'd know how quickly her responsibilities would be over and she could make her plans accordingly. She'd have the money from this job to give her time to find the next one.

"Shall we go down to the main room and go over your selections?" Caroline asked, picking up her notebook.

Stella eyed Danny. "Isn't Felicia going to watch him?"

"Not today," Caroline answered smoothly.

"Why not?" Stella asked in her usual forthright manner. "Is something the matter?

"No, not at all."

"I know Felicia can seem a little eccentric at times," Stella persisted.

Caroline decided not to go there. "She's very good at relating to children, I can see that."

"She's spoiled Cassie, that's for sure," Stella said flatly. Caroline avoided commenting as she handed Danny a tablet and a pencil. "You can be my helper. We'll draw pictures, okay?"

"No bears in the room?" he protested, wide-eyed.

"No bears," she reassured him. Thank heavens, the antler chandelier didn't seem to bother him.

"I'm with him," Stella said, obviously hiding a smile. "And we're not going to put up any mangy old trophies on our walls, are we, Danny?"

He solemnly shook his head.

As they looked over the main room, Caroline suggested to Stella that they visualize the space as empty—empty of furniture, shutters, pictures, rug and all hangings.

The morning flew by and Caroline was delighted with the progress they made blocking out conversational areas. Two brocaded wingback chairs and a coffee table were to be placed in front of the windows overlooking the lake. Three large burgundy sofas were chosen to be placed in a U-shape in front of the huge fireplace for a conversational setting. Caroline recommended selecting wooden cornices for the tall windows and removing the shutters which would allow more natural light into the high-ceilinged room.

They discussed other possibilities at lunch and had just returned to the main room when Wes interrupted a conversation about wall hangings.

"What do you think, Wes? See anything you

like?" Stella asked in a tone which indicated she knew who would be paying the price tag. She handed him photos of various art treatments recommended for large wall areas.

"I like the picture Danny drew," he said evasively as he picked up Danny's tablet showing a stick figure of a boy and a weird-looking horse complete with saddle and reins. "That would look great on any wall."

"You can have it," Danny said quickly.

Caroline smothered a chuckle. She knew her son would be expecting to find it displayed the next time he visited Wes's suite.

"Thank you very much," Wes said solemnly. "Let's leave it in your tablet for now. You may want to make a whole book of drawings for me to chose from."

Nicely done, Caroline thought, pleased with the way Wes was dealing with her son. Without Cassie around, he was paying a lot more attention to Danny.

"How would you like to go sledding this afternoon, Danny?"

Caroline's smile quickly faded. "Oh, I'm afraid that's not a good idea. Stella and I are really making headway. I'm afraid we're going to be at it for several more hours."

"Oh, I wasn't planning on interrupting your work. I'm sure I can handle both of the kids myself."

"They don't have to go far," Stella quickly assured Caroline. "There's a small slope close to the lodge."

"You can watch from the front windows if you like," Wes told her, obviously a little irritated at her protective manner.

Danny tugged on her arm. "Please...please."

Even as she hesitated, she realized that she really had no basis for refusing. After all, one parent supervising the activity was all that was needed.

"All right."

"Yippee!" He grabbed Wes's hand. "Let's go."

Wes laughed. "First, you change into some warm clothes. I'll go tell Cassie." He smiled at Caroline. "Say twenty minutes. I'll meet Danny back here."

Caroline was thankful Danny's snowsuit had been at the cleaners when the fire had destroyed their house. After putting on knitted cap, gloves and boots, he was ready and they returned to the main room.

Danny waited impatiently and kept looking out a front window as if he was afraid they'd leave without him.

"Through the years, the lodge has collected all kinds of accumulated sleds, ice skates, tubes and rubber rafts," Stella told Caroline. "Believe me, they've been tested by kids of every size and age. Wes will find the right sled for Danny, don't worry."

"He can't use mine," Cassie piped up as she came into the room with Wes. She looked like a snow bunny in a white furry hat and matching white snowsuit and boots.

"He gets the Red Flyer," Wes said quickly. "It's the best one for a boy." He'd changed to gray ski pants, a matching parka, gloves and snowboots. "Come on, let's go. Tim is bringing the sleds around to the front."

The two children bounded out of the house ahead of him. Caroline and Stella watched them through a front window and saw Wes give each of the children a sled to pull, taking the largest one for himself.

They tromped through the snow to a place where the ground sloped gently down to a meadow bordering the lake. As they made their first run down the hill, Caroline wished she'd dropped everything and gone with them. Danny was laughing as he bounded off his sled and began pulling it back up the slope for another run. She was relieved that Wes was making sure they made their downhill runs one by one so there wouldn't be any collisions.

Stella turned away from the window. "Let's get back to work. We'll make out the orders for the furniture and materials and then call it a day. I want to think about the room accessories. I am still undecided about an area rug."

They'd been working only a few minutes when they heard the sound of a car engine outside.

"That's probably Dexter coming back from Telluride," Stella said. "I wonder why he didn't drive around back to the garage like always?" She looked out the window. "Damn," she swore.

"What is it?"

"Company."

Caroline moved to the window. Dexter was holding the car door open for an attractive, stylish young woman with red hair.

"Who's that?" Caroline asked.

"Nicole Kitridge. Her family owns half the mining interests in these mountains. She and

Wes had a thing going last year. Bets were down that Nicole would become the next Mrs. Wesley Wainwright," Stella said with an edge to her voice.

"What happened?"

Stella shrugged. "Who knows? There were plenty of wealthy men lined up for her attention. Personally, I think it was jealousy on Wes's part. He can't stand competition in any form, which stands him in good stead in the business world but it wears thin in a personal relationship."

Nicole must have seen Wes because she immediately headed in that direction. As Nicole reached him and the two embraced, Stella said dryly, "I guess they made up."

"Apparently they have." Caroline remembered Wes saying he and Dexter were late getting back from Telluride the last time because they'd spent time with some friends. She wondered if Nicole was the real reason.

Dexter joined the couple and they watched Danny and Cassie take a couple of runs down the slope.

"They're coming in," Stella said, smoothing back her hair and pulling down her knit sweater.

Caroline watched at the window as the group turned toward the lodge. The woman helped Danny pull his sled, Dexter took Cassie's and Wes pulled his own. When they reached the lodge, Wes was laughing at something Nicole said and Caroline was foolishly annoyed by the obvious harmony between them.

When they came into the room, Stella greeted the visitor with an effusive, "How nice to see you, Nicole."

Caroline deliberately gave all her attention to Danny. "Did you have fun, honey?" she asked as she helped him take off his snowy jacket. "Your cheeks are rosy."

"I went down the hill—really fast," he bragged.

"Me, too," Cassie piped up. "Didn't I, Daddy?"

"Yes, indeed," Wes assured her. "Both of you are ready for the junior Olympics."

Danny pointed at Nicole. "She won a medal. She told me. A real one…for bobby-sledding." He frowned when they all laughed.

"What fun to be here." Nicole smiled at Wes as she unbuttoned her fur-trimmed, green suede coat. Wispy red curls framed her face and a hint of freckles dotted her perky nose. "When Dexter offered to drive me here for a visit, I just couldn't refuse."

"Always at your service," Dexter replied with mock gallantry as he quickly took her coat and laid it on a nearby chair.

As Nicole's gray-blue eyes traveled to Caroline, Wes quickly introduced her. "Caroline Fairchild. She's our interior decorator. Stella has her busy with all sorts of plans for the lodge."

"Yes, Dexter told me. It's quite a challenging project, I would imagine," she commented as she glanced at the pile of material and books.

"We're just in the exploring stage," Stella said quickly as if she didn't want Nicole putting in her two cents' worth.

Dexter shifted impatiently. "Why don't we all have something to warm us up?"

"Good idea," Wes agreed as if he was uncomfortable with the women's chatter.

"Come on, Stella," Dexter urged. "Let's see what we can wrestle up in the kitchen for a snack."

Wes took Cassie's hand. "We'll get a fire going in the social room."

"It's no fun in the house," she complained. "Why can't we go out and make a snowman?"

"Maybe later," he answered shortly as they disappeared down the hall.

Caroline would rather have excused herself, but she didn't know how to manage it without seeming rude. She was surprised when Nicole fell into step beside her and Danny as they followed Wes and Cassie.

"You have a darling little boy," she told Caroline as she beamed at Danny.

"He's very special," Caroline agreed and squeezed his hand.

"I bet Wes is enjoying having him around. Men are really partial to boys, aren't they?"

"Oh, I don't know. Every child is very special. Wes certainly loves his daughter and they seem to have a very close relationship."

"Perhaps, but there's a sad loneliness in him that all his money and prestige can't seem to fill. He clearly has a deep longing for more family. He ought to get married and have more kids."

"All redheads?" Caroline couldn't believe her own ears and was mortified she'd spoken aloud. Deciding the best defense was offense, she added quickly, "Stella told me you and Wes were an item. I was just guessing there might be a wedding in the future."

Nicole measured Caroline with her steady

gray-blue eyes. "Do I detect some personal interest in his future plans?"

"Only that I wish him well," Caroline said evenly. "He seems deserving of happiness."

"One way or another Wes usually gets what he wants," Nicole said thoughtfully. "Once he makes up his mind."

Caroline had the good sense just to smile and keep her mouth shut. She was glad there wasn't opportunity for further exchanges.

Wes and Dexter monopolized Nicole's attention while Stella served hot drinks and freshly baked muffins. Caroline sat on the sofa between the two children. Nicole was a vivacious conversationalist and the adult talk centered on people and events Caroline had never heard about. It was obvious that Dexter was enamored with the attractive redhead and he did his best to be charming.

In contrast, Wes gave his attention to building up the fire and seemed rather preoccupied. He kept looking at his watch and when Tim Henderson poked his head into the room, Wes swung around with a questioning look on his face.

Tim nodded. "That call you've been waiting for is on the line."

"Good." He turned to Nicole. "Excuse me, I have some business matters to take care of. You'll be staying the night, of course?"

"If there's room in the lodge," she replied in a coquettish tone.

"I think we can find one," he said rather briskly.

Caroline was surprised when he shot her a quick look before he hurried out of the room. The sudden hardness in his eyes made him a stranger and she felt an invading chill in the warm room.

WES SHUT the door to his office before he sat down and punched the blinking button on his phone. When Delio identified himself, Wes said curtly, "I've been waiting for your call."

"I flew into Denver on a red-eye last night. I could tell you were impatient for a report so I covered as much ground as I could today." He paused, as if searching for the right words.

"What did you find out?" Wes demanded impatiently.

"I'm not sure."

"What in the hell does that mean?" Wes could summon extreme patience when handling business matters, but something personal was a different story.

"It means I didn't find anything. Nada!"

"Why not?" Wes's tone indicated the fault must lie with the investigator.

"Because there's no official record of any adoption by Thomas and Caroline Fairchild."

Wes's hand was suddenly sweaty on the telephone receiver. "You're sure?"

"If the supposed adoption took place, it wasn't registered with the State of Colorado."

A jolt went through Wes as if someone had landed a punch in the middle of his stomach. No adoption?

"Apparently the husband located the baby and arranged for all the legal work," Wes told him.

"What was the name of the lawyer who handled the legal forms?"

"I don't know."

"Can't you get me a name?" Delio pressured. "I could check that way and might be able to come up with something that makes sense."

"I'll try. I need more information to know what the real story is."

"That's wise," Delio admitted. His tone held a warning. "Innocent or not, Wes, we need to handle this very carefully."

"I understand," Wes answered as a heaviness settled in his chest. He didn't want to hurt anyone. He just wanted his son back. He felt guilty treating Caroline with such deceit, but he had no choice. Until he knew the truth, he couldn't let his feelings get in the way. "I'll try to get more information as quickly as I can."

"In the meantime, Wes, I'll gather as much personal history on both Thomas and Caroline Fairchild as I can, undercover. Since the husband was in the medical field, I should be able to find plenty of people who knew him. Interrogating coworkers might uncover someone who can verify the source of the adopted baby. It could be that everything was on the up and up, despite the lack of Colorado records and I'll get some leads that will answer our questions."

"He graduated from the University of Colorado," Wes offered. "That's where he met his wife. She was raised in eastern Colorado and both parents are dead."

"How did you meet her?"

"My sister-in-law brought her to the lodge. She's an interior decorator." Wes realized then how little he really knew about Caroline even though she had touched him in ways that were deeply personal.

He couldn't allow any feelings to detract him. Not now, when there was a chance that a little boy with curved pink toes might be his own flesh and blood.

Chapter Eleven

Wes had not returned from his telephone call by the time the children had finished their hot chocolate and Felicia had come for Cassie. Nicole was happily entertaining Dexter and Tim with a flirtatious story that had brought a frown to Stella's face when Caroline made her excuses and left with Danny.

They had made their way upstairs to the second floor and Caroline was just opening their door when Wes came out of his suite at the far end of the corridor.

Danny bolted away from her and ran down the hall to meet him.

"Can we make a snowman now? Can we?" he begged with childish impatience.

Wes laughed and took his hand as they walked toward Caroline. "Let's wait for more snow. Then we can make a really big one."

"How big?" Danny asked with rounded eyes.

"One so tall you'll have to stand on a ladder to put on his ugly nose," he promised.

Danny giggled as if he was already imagining the snowman's funny face.

Wes's smile faded when they reached her, and Caroline wondered why he seemed so guarded. "I'm sorry. Is Danny pestering you again?"

"Not at all," he answered quickly. "In fact, I'd like to spend more time with him."

"I'm sure he'd like that. Danny's always on the go and I'm afraid that sometimes all that bouncing energy gets him into trouble."

"He just needs someone to give him more attention."

She raised an eyebrow. Where did this over-involved businessman get off telling her what her son needed? She didn't like his dictatorial tone and bristled at his unwarranted criticism.

"I rather think he may be getting too much attention. He doesn't have much competition for my time." She paused for emphasis. "No pressing business and social obligations."

Nicole's vivacious voice suddenly floated down the hall as if to punctuate Caroline's last remarks. "There you are, Wes, darling. I wondered if you were lost to us forever."

When she reached them, she looped her arm through his. "Stella didn't seem to know where to put my overnight things."

Without looking at either of them, Caroline said to Danny, "Let's get you a warm bath."

She wasn't about to stand in the hall while Nicole and Wes discussed their sleeping arrangements. She took his hand and closed the door behind them.

"Why are you mad, Mommy?" Danny asked

as she helped him bathe and dress to go downstairs to dinner.

"I'm not mad."

"He's a nice man, Cassie's dad. Isn't he?"

"Yes, of course," she answered quickly.

"Then why don't you like him?"

"I do." *Your mother's jealous.* Somehow, the silent admission made her feel better.

All right, so she was physically attracted to Wes Wainwright. She straightened and firmed her shoulders. That didn't mean she couldn't rein in any serious romantic feelings for him. No telling how many romantic partners of his had crossed the threshold of his mountain retreat. Obviously, he and Nicole knew how to play the game. Her best bet was to give them both wide clearance while she did the job she'd been hired to do.

When she and Danny went downstairs to dinner, her defenses were up but Wes and Nicole didn't show. *Probably having dinner in his suite,* she thought, rather wistfully. Her longing to be with him challenged her pride. She'd been foolish enough to respond to his sexual charm. Just remembering the feel of his mouth on hers sent a rippling of desire through her.

When Stella joined her and Danny at their table, Caroline had trouble keeping her imagination free of thoughts about what was happening upstairs. She had to force herself to focus on what Stella was saying and pretend to be receptive to her instructions.

"We'll spend the morning clearing out the main room and getting rid of all the collected bric-a-brac, newspapers, magazines and such that has collected over the years," she told Caroline in her employer tone. "That way we'll have all clean shelves and tables for new purchases."

As Stella continued with a litany of plans for new lamps, accessories and rugs, Caroline nodded without comment. She knew Stella well enough by now to know she wasn't asking for any two-way discussion about the new purchases.

As soon as they had finished eating, Caroline made her escape, after promising to meet Stella at nine o'clock the next morning.

A growing discontent stayed with her even after she'd tucked Danny in bed. She lay stiffly looking up at the ceiling, trying to forget the strange way Wes had looked at her just before Nicole arrived and slipped her arm through his.

The warm blankets failed to quell a sudden chill as she remembered the way his eyes had narrowed when he looked at her. It was almost as if he were judging her in some way and finding her lacking.

THE NEXT MORNING the feeling of discontent was even stronger. Caroline awoke with a knowing that permeated her total awareness.

It's time to leave.

Logically, the intuitive decision made no sense. Nothing had changed in her finances. The insurance company was still marking time about settling. She had no assurance she would be paid for the time she'd already devoted to the redecorating plans. Still, a nameless urgency flowed through her like the swift current of a river.

As soon as they were dressed, Caroline hurried Danny downstairs to the telephone in the hall alcove. She dialed Betty McClure's number and was relieved when her friend answered with her familiar, "Hello, Betty speaking."

"I was afraid you might have already left for the store," Caroline said quickly.

"Caroline! How in the world are you? We've been dying to know how the mountain project is going."

"I'm sorry, I didn't call sooner. It's…it's been a challenge."

"Oh, what kind?"

Caroline almost laughed. Such a simple question but such a tangled answer. "I'll try to explain later. At the moment, I'm wondering if there have been any other inquires about my services. I could be back and on another decorating job by the beginning of next week."

"My goodness. You're not going to finish the Wainwright contract? Is it really that bad?" she prodded. "It sounded like such a wonderful opportunity."

"It's complicated," Caroline answered quickly. She couldn't make sense of all of it herself, let alone try to explain to someone else the undefined urgency that had overtaken her.

"Well, I'm really sorry. Gosh, I don't know what to tell you. People aren't in the mood to redecorate this time of year," Betty reminded her. "You know how it is. Come springtime, Caroline, you'll probably have plenty of work. The Wainwright recommendation would be invaluable, you know."

Caroline took a deep breath even as her hand tightened on the phone receiver. She knew her friend was right. Defaulting on this job was irresponsible. And letting her feelings for Wes Wainwright dictate her career choices was juvenile. Financially, she could not afford to just pack up and go back—and to what?

"I guess I'd better give it more thought," she admitted reluctantly. "Thanks for the counseling session."

"Anytime. What are friends for? I know this is a rough time for you. Have you heard from the insurance company?"

"Not much. Only that an arson investigation is holding up settlement. Apparently there's some question about whether I burned down my own house to collect."

Betty muttered a swear word. "Hang in there. They can't dally forever." Her tone brightened. "I've been looking at some homes in our area that would be perfect for you and Danny. With the money you're going to get from the lodge contract, you'll be able to move into something even nicer than you had. Keep the faith."

After Caroline hung up, she realized Betty was right. She shouldn't let nebulous feelings dictate decisions that lacked definite validity. Maybe she should have shared her tangled feelings about Wes? She needed someone to tell her how big a fool she was.

During Caroline's talk with Betty, Danny had been playing with Cassie's pretend telephone. When she heard him ordering a pizza with everything, she smothered a smile.

"Does that mean you're hungry and ready for breakfast?" she teased.

"Is that what we're having? Pizza?" he asked, hopefully.

"Probably not," Caroline admitted. "But something just as good, I bet."

Danny looked skeptical.

Caroline braced herself against the possibility of finding Wes and Nicole having breakfast together, but there was no sign of either of them in the room. She realized then that they were probably having a private breakfast in his suite.

Dexter was the only one seated at a table. After she and Danny filled their plates and moved away from the buffet, he stood up and held out a chair for her at his table.

She couldn't bring herself to intentionally snub him. As it turned out, she was glad that she hadn't. The conversation was very enlightening.

"I'm taking Nicole back to Telluride this morning," he told her.

"So soon?" she asked in what she hoped was a casual tone.

"Yep. Apparently, her single room last night wasn't to her liking—if you get what I mean." Dexter winked suggestively. "Too bad. I guess Wes wasn't in the mood for company."

Caroline's heartbeat suddenly quickened.

Deliberately, she gave her attention to helping Danny cut up his slice of ham. Her outward lack of interest didn't seem to deter Dexter in the least.

"Nothing so dead as an old love, I guess," he continued in his gossipy manner. "They made a nice couple but Nicole certainly doesn't need his money. Not like some of the women who chase after him." His pudgy smile included Caroline. "I think Wes gets a little bored with all the feminine attention." He sighed. "Ah, if I could be so lucky."

"What do you do for a living? Or do you?" Caroline asked pointedly. She was irritated with his insulting innuendoes.

Dexter chuckled as if he was amused by her directness. "You might say my business is entertaining myself. My dear papa left me enough bucks to enjoy life and I intend to do it handsomely." He looked at her over the rim of his coffee cup. "I bet you've never

really let yourself go, Caroline. Maybe surrendered to some wild joy just because you
felt like it?"

"No, I haven't," she answered honestly.

"Maybe you ought to try it."

"Some of us don't have that luxury," she
countered rather impatiently. "My father left
me a dry land farm, mortgaged to the hilt. On
the other hand, he left me something more important. The strength to make it on my own."

"I admit I've been lucky," Dex admitted, the
meaning of her jab missing him entirely. "Really
lucky to have friends like Wes. He's been the
most important person in my life. To be truthful,
I'm glad he and Nicole didn't connect this time."
He looked a little sheepish. "I admit I get a little
jealous when he gives too much of his attention
to someone else. On the other hand, I don't like
it when I see him unhappy."

"Is he unhappy?"

"I reckon so. He saddled up Prince early this

morning for a solitary ride. Wes does that when he's got a problem to solve. He likes to get away and think it through. Something's bothering him. Do you know what it is?"

"Why don't you ask him?" Caroline countered evenly.

"He's almost as tight-lipped as you are. Well, I guess I'll have to wait and see if what I suspect is going on under my nose." He pushed back his plate and stood up. "I've got to get Nicole's luggage and bring the SUV around. She wants to have breakfast on the way. My guess is the lady's pride is hurt and she wants out of here before Wes gets back."

Caroline nodded without comment.

"Will you tell Wes that I may decide to spend the night in Telluride, consoling the lady and all that?" Without giving her a chance to refuse the role of messenger, he got up and sauntered out of the room.

As Caroline poured herself another cup of

coffee from the table carafe, she thoughtfully digested the information Dexter had given her.

Wes had not spent the night making love to Nicole.

The tightness in her heart eased. She had imagined him touching Nicole with his soft trailing fingers and igniting her flesh with heat. Now, she knew his lips had not played upon hers with the inviting promise of a lover's caress and—

"What's the matter, Mommy?" Danny peered up at her with the curiosity of a six-year-old. "You look funny."

Caroline smiled as she brushed down a wayward tuft of his hair. "Are you about through with your breakfast? Finish your cereal and you can have one of those choco- late doughnuts."

As Danny attacked the oatmeal, she leaned back in her chair and gazed out the window.

The view of the snow-covered ground and

lake was like a winter postcard with a clearing blue sky and dazzling shafts of morning sunlight splaying through the snow-laden branches. She blinked at the brightness and was about to look away when a dark, fast-moving horse and rider came into view. She quickly set down her coffee cup.

Wes! He was heading for the stable.

Just then Cassie and Felicia came into the room. When the little girl saw Danny, she ran over to the table. "Goody. We're going to eat with you."

"I'm going to have a doughnut," Danny said as if that somehow put him ahead.

"Me, too."

Caroline stood up when Felicia and Cassie were ready to sit down at the table. "Felicia, will you keep an eye on Danny for a few minutes? I have something I need to do."

"Yes, of course. We've been missing Danny, haven't we, Cassie?" She seemed relieved that

Caroline had decided to leave him with her. "Take your time."

"I won't be long," Caroline promised as she quickly left the room. Even though she was wearing a heavy sweater, warm slacks and her walking boots, she shivered at the onslaught of crisp air that hit her as she left the lodge.

By the time she got to the stables, Wes had already unsaddled Prince. Without him noticing she lingered in the doorway and watched as he threw a blanket over the stallion and began rubbing down his glistening black hide.

The bond between man and horse was unmistakable as his hands moved gracefully over the horse's shoulders, thighs, lower legs and rump. A deep caring and an outward expression of love was evident in his every stroke.

As Caroline watched him, a warm stirring of sexual desire crept through her. Every movement of his body was a tantalizing promise of his commanding masculinity. As his hands traveled the warm contours of the stallion's body, she felt his gentle strokes on her own skin. She'd never felt that kind of instant desire before. An aching need that rose full-blown and demanding brought beads of perspiration to her brow.

She should leave, walk out the door. Cool the physical desire sluicing hotly through her. It was insanity to want this man so passionately. An exhilarating kind of madness. Not at all like her usual self-contained person.

She must have made a sound that swung him around to face the door. When he saw her, his expression was one of surprise. For a moment she thought he was going to roughly demand what she was doing there. As his gaze traveled over her, his shoulders seemed to relax and his frown eased. "Well, hello. You're too late for a ride this morning."

"That's too bad," she replied in the same even tone. Now that she was face to face with him she couldn't think of anything suitable to say. She fell back on the excuse Dexter had given her.

"I had breakfast with Dex and he wanted me to tell you he was taking Nicole back to Telluride this morning in the SUV." She watched his expression and his eyes narrowed slightly.

Without comment, he turned back to the stallion and finished currying him before he put him in his stall.

They walked back to the house, side by side, and the total content of his conversation was about the weather and early warnings of another snowstorm. Somehow, their former easy companionship had completely vanished.

Once inside the main room of the lodge, Caroline decided that she needed to make a few things clear to him. "I know Stella is going to be upset, but I'm considering breaking my contract with her."

"You can't leave!" He stared at her as if

she'd hit him in the middle of the stomach and he couldn't get his breath.

"I have another job lined up," she lied gibbly. "I would appreciate receiving a fair compensation for the work I've already done."

He just stared at her as if his thoughts were whirling like an off-balance gyroscope. "No."

For a foolish moment, she thought he was going to declare some deep feelings for her. His eyes fastened on her with the force of a grappling hook as he put his hands on her arms.

"I can't let you go."

The words were right but there was no lover's caress in his tone. His angry demeanor made her pull away from him.

He ran an agitated hand through his hair. "We…we have to talk. Please. There's something you have to know."

His manner warned her it wasn't something inconsequential. As her heartbeat quickened, she asked, "What is it? Tell me."

"Not here." He sent a furtive look around the room as if someone might have been watching the emotional scene.

"I need to get back to Danny. I left him with Felicia eating breakfast."

"He'll be fine. Nobody will be in the reading room this time of morning." He grabbed her hand and pulled her down the hall.

Once inside the room, he shut the door and motioned for her to have a seat on the couch. He seemed undecided whether he should sit down beside her or remain standing. He ended up leaning against the library table and looking down at her.

"Do you remember the afternoon we spent watching the kids in the Jacuzzi?"

She nodded.

"You left to go to the laundry room, remember?" He seemed to run out of breath for a moment. "Well, something happened while you were gone."

She stiffened. "Was it something you should have told me about?" At the time she'd been puzzled by the change in him when she returned to the room.

"I probably should have, but I wasn't sure of anything then." His mouth tightened. "You hadn't told me Danny was adopted. At least not until later."

"What does that have to do with anything?" Her voice was suddenly sharper than she intended. Something deep inside registered an unnamed danger when he hesitated to answer her question.

"The boy has the same physical characteristics in his toes as my father, grandfather and other members of the Wainwright family."

She stared at him blankly.

"Don't you see? My infant son was kidnapped when he was only a month old. Already his tiny feet showed the family's trait of curved little toes."

"What are you saying?"

"It's conceivable that you have adopted my baby boy who was taken from our nursery six years ago."

His words stunned her. Not because she found them valid. She couldn't believe that he'd come to such a ludicrous conclusion. She'd judged him to be an intelligent and perceptive man and was appalled that a longing for his own son had twisted his cognitive reasoning in such a bizarre way. Caroline felt a deep sympathy for him.

"It's certainly a coincidence," she admitted gently. "And I can see why any physical similarities to your own family would be startling. But these things do happen. Danny's birth mother or father must have passed along an aberration that resembled yours. It's as simple as that."

"Maybe not as simple as you think," he argued. "What do you know about the birth mother?"

His sharp question took her back for a moment. "Not very much, really. She was a young unmarried woman—"

"Did you meet her?"

"No, Thomas handled everything about the adoption. He and the lawyer took care of all the legal business."

"And this took place in Denver, Colorado." At her nod, he added, "What would you say if I told you there is no record of such an adoption?"

"I would say you're misinformed." A swell of anger brought a hot flush to her face. "Have you been looking into Danny's adoption without my knowledge?"

"Yes, I hired a reputable private detective, Clyde Delio, to look into the adoption." His eyes bit into hers. "Caroline, Delio can't find any adoption registered in your name in the state of Colorado."

"Then I think you should fire him," she flared as she stood up. "I have Danny's official adoption papers in a metal box I saved from the fire. I'll go to my car and get them. That ought to prove how wrong you are." And with that, she practically ran out of the room.

Chapter Twelve

Wes laid the papers out on his desk and Caroline watched as he examined every word, line, paragraph and signature.

She could not believe this was happening!

He was trying to claim her son!

She felt sick to her stomach realizing how he'd played her for a fool. Plying her with wine and caresses, he'd encouraged her most private confidences until she'd told him what he wanted to know—Danny was adopted. He had hired a private investigator without even a hint of his intentions.

Her eyes stung with threatening tears as a mixture of anger and hurt swept over her. She hated him for deceiving her, for letting her believe that he really cared for her. Now she knew the bitter truth. His attention to her had been a calculated means to achieving his own ends.

Was this what Felicia was trying to warn her about? Caroline had viewed the nanny's behavior as eccentric, but maybe Wes had gone off the deep end like this before. Did any male child who was his lost son's age come under this kind of scrutiny? Maybe Felicia had seen signs that Wes had become fixated on Danny. Caroline had noticed Wes had a genuine liking for her son, but now it appeared that his interest had been something deeper and threatening.

Well, she'd made enough of a fool of herself. Better to have discovered his real intentions now rather than later. She folded her arms and waited impatiently until he finally finished looking at the papers and put them down.

"Satisfied?"

"They seem authentic."

"They *are* authentic!" she snapped.

As she reached for them, he stopped her hand. "May I make some copies?"

A dark, guarded solemnity had settled in his eyes and he seemed like a total stranger. Was this the same man who had held her tenderly in his arms?

"What for?"

"I'd like my investigator to take a look at them."

"A waste of time and money, but I guess you have plenty of that," she jabbed.

"I just have to be sure." His eyes held a haunted look. "Damn sure."

She started to refuse because of the bitterness she felt inside. Even with concrete evidence in front of him, he was refusing to accept the truth. Only the need to settle his obsession as soon as possible made her decide to let him copy the papers.

"Where's your copier?" She wasn't about to let the papers out of her sight.

Because his suite office seemed fully equipped, she wasn't surprised when he pointed to one on a nearby stand.

"All right. Let's settle this once and for all."

She stood closely by his side and watched as he fed the papers into the machine. She was prepared for any trickery and took them away from him as he made a copy of each one. Once the adoption papers were back in her hands, she turned on her heels to leave.

"Caroline!" He stopped her before she reached the door. "Please understand—"

"Oh, I do!" She swung around and faced him. "I understand perfectly. You've exploited my feelings to gain the information you wanted. Now you have it and the charade is over! Once your investigator verifies the adoption papers I'll leave with my son and trust that I'll never see you again." Turning her back on him, she fought back tears as she fled down the hall.

WES IMMEDIATELY CALLED Delio and alerted him that he was faxing copies of the Fairchild adoption papers to him at his hotel.

"Where'd they come from?"

"The mother had copies."

"I'll be damned."

Wes would have suspected a slipshod job if it had been anybody but Delio. He was too damn good. There had to be a logical explanation why the private dectective had missed the papers.

"George Goodman is the lawyer's name on the papers. As far as I can tell everything looks in order. As soon as you've checked them out, get back to me."

"Will do."

Wes's hand was sweaty as he hung up. Waiting for anything or anybody had never been his strong point. He'd always been a doer, but what kind of action could he take in a situation like this?

Caroline's hurt and outrage weighed heavily with him. All the years of passion and desire that had lain dormant since Pamela's death had exploded into feelings he hadn't known he still had. Somehow, she had touched him in vulnerable areas he'd always kept protected from other women. It hurt deeply to see the scathing look in her eyes, but it couldn't be helped. He had to know the truth! The need to verify Danny's parentage outweighed everything else.

He was glad he'd kept Nicole at a distance during her surprise visit. She'd tried her best to renew their early romantic fling, but playing games with her was the last thing on his mind.

When Caroline checked on Danny in the dining room, she found Felicia had taken him with Cassie to her apartment after breakfast.

The door was ajar and as Caroline went in,

she saw that the two children were playing some kind of dice game.

"I'm winning," Danny bragged when he saw his mother. "Can't I stay?"

"Please let him," Cassie begged.

"We've been missing Danny," Felicia said, adding to the chorus as she rose from her nearby chair. "And you, too."

As her penetrating gaze settled on Caroline, she asked, "Is something the matter? I sense turbulence in your spirit."

"I'm not sure *turbulence* is the right word. *Fury* might come closer," Caroline muttered with tight lips.

"Perhaps you'd like to stay for a cup of my tansy tea?" Felicia offered quickly.

Caroline suspected the invitation was for more than sipping tea. Undoubtedly, Felicia would direct the conversation to satisfy her curiosity. Well, two could play that game. Caroline had a few questions of her own.

Besides, she was in no mood to face Stella in the workroom.

"Yes, I think I would like a cup of tea, Felicia. Thank you."

Felicia quickly set out cups on the kitchen table and prepared a pot of a fragrant scented tea. She allowed Caroline a few minutes of quiet contemplation before she sat down and remarked pointedly, "Your aura is a worrisome gray this morning."

Caroline managed a weak smile. "Gray? Not a fiery red?"

Felicia handed Caroline a cup. "This will help."

Under other circumstances Caroline might have enjoyed the unique taste of the tea but she had too much on her mind. "Felicia, I need to talk about something that I know must be painful for you. I wouldn't do it if I had any other choice."

"It's all right. I gave up being offended a long time ago," she replied quietly. "It's Wes, isn't it?"

"How did you know?"

"The vibrations between the two of you are hard to miss."

Caroline moistened her lips. "I need to know about the kidnapping. What did Wes do to try and recover the baby boy?"

Felicia didn't seemed the least bit surprised by the question. "Everything humanly possible," she answered readily. "The kidnappers could have named their ransom and Wes would have gladly paid it. He offered an enormous reward, hired a fleet of detectives and followed up every possible lead. Nothing."

"No suspects at all?"

"None. Even the FBI failed to come up with any viable leads."

"Surely they must have had some suspects."

"Wes had plenty of competitors who were jealous of his growing financial empire. The kidnapping could have been in retaliation by some revengeful investor." She paused as she took another sip of tea. "But I don't think so."

"Then who?"

Staring at her cup, Felicia slowly twirled the liquid. "I've asked that question for nearly seven years. Someday we'll know." She leaned over and patted Caroline's hand. "You have to be kind to him."

Caroline jerked her hand away. "He's trying to claim my son."

Felicia didn't say anything for a long moment. "I don't understand. What do you mean by claim? If he wants to help you raise your son—"

"No, that's not it at all. He's trying to claim Danny as his own."

Felicia listened intently as Caroline told her about the family resemblance, the investigator Wes had hired and his report that no record of Danny's adoption existed.

Felicia's eyes rounded. "You mean—"

"The investigator's report is a bunch of

crap!" Caroline retorted with an unladylike word. "Danny's adoption was totally legal."

"Are you certain?" A sudden glow brightened her dark eyes. "Maybe—"

"No!" Caroline snapped and then drew in a deep breath to settle her voice. "My son's birth mother was a young unmarried woman and my husband and lawyer handled the adoption. I have copies of the legal adoption and I showed them to Wes. He's going to send copies to his investigator and that will be the end of that!"

Felicia's expression changed and Caroline knew she would have preferred for Wes and his investigator to be right. Undoubtedly everyone at the lodge would line up against her when they learned of Wes's interest in Danny.

Caroline pushed away the teacup. "I have to go."

As she stood, she felt a little unsteady on her

feet. Placing her hands on the table, she braced herself as her legs threatened to give way.

"You'd best sit down," Felicia said quietly. "Tansy tea has that effect on some people."

"Then why did you give it to me?" Caroline asked in an accusing tone.

"Because you needed it. Now sit down and collect yourself. You'll not do yourself any good chasing phantoms of your imagination."

"It's not me who's imagining things." She sank back in the chair and put her heavy head in her hands to hold it up. "I can't believe any of this."

"You've fallen in love with him, haven't you? I knew I should have warned you. Poor Wes, he doesn't have a heart to give to a woman. Pamela broke it before she died."

"Didn't she love him?"

"As much as she could, I guess."

"It wasn't a happy marriage?"

"Wes gave and she took," Felicia said sadly.

"Even with all the attention and flattery that came Pamela's way as a beauty queen, she never had enough love to share with anyone." She eyed Caroline. "He's very protective of Cassie, as you can understand. If there's a chance that Danny is his…"

"There isn't!"

Caroline rose to her feet again and this time the adrenaline rushing through her body seemed to counteract the effects of the tansy tea.

She left the kitchen. "Come on, Danny, we have to go."

"Can Cassie come, too? We could play games while you work."

"Can I? Can I?" she begged.

Caroline waited for Felicia to tell the little girl no, but she didn't. "If it's all right with Danny's mother," she said smiling in that secretive way of hers.

Caroline silently groaned. She didn't feel up to battling all three of them so she gave in. "If they'll amuse themselves, I guess it will be okay. Stella and I are going to be cleaning out the main room."

Felicia quickly gathered up a few toys and games for them to take along. "I'll come and get Cassie in a couple of hours," she promised.

Stella was already in the main room. She frowned when she saw Caroline had the two children with her. "Is Felicia ill?"

"No."

"Then why are the children with you?"

"They won't be any trouble," Caroline said, avoiding a direct answer. She had too much on her mind to argue about watching the kids for a couple of hours. As quickly as she could she settled them on the rug in the corner of the room. "Play nicely."

Stella had decided to tag all the furniture she wanted removed. "I'll have Tim put everything in the storage room until we decide what to do with it. Maybe we'll find a secondhand dealer in

Telluride to haul it away. Right now, we'll have to clean out all the drawers and cabinets. There's a lot of family stuff that Wes will want to save."

Under other circumstances, Caroline might have enjoyed looking through boxes of old photographs and yellowed newspaper clippings. There were even bundles of letters handwritten by members of the Wainwright family.

In Caroline's state of mind, every piece of memorabilia looked threatening because it seemed to contain a warning that this rich, powerful family took what they wanted when they wanted it.

"Daddy!" Cassie leaped to her feet and ran across the room as Wes came in. "Come play with us."

Caroline kept her gaze on the pile of photograph albums and avoided looking in the direction of the doorway.

"Oh, good, Wes, I have a job for you. We want to get this room cleared out. I was just going to get Tim and Shane. You can help them move some of this stuff."

"My lucky day," Wes replied dryly. "I think I'd rather play games with the kids."

"I'm winning," Danny announced proudly.

"I won the first one," Cassie bragged.

Wes laughed. "Well, you two are too good for me. I think I'd better help pack boxes."

Stella made some under-her-breath remark as she left to summon her son and Tim. Caroline stiffened when Wes eased down on the rug beside her.

"What's all this stuff?" he asked, pointing to the boxes she was filling.

"The kinds of things a family collects through the years."

"Oh, I recognize some of the photograph books," he said as he took one out of a box and began turning the pages.

He was sitting so close to her that their shoulders almost brushed as he began turning the pages. The familiar scent of his warm body assaulted her. She knew that any friendly overtures on his part were nothing but a calculated strategy to camouflage his real interest—her son!

"Look at that." Chuckling, he pointed to a photograph of a grinning young boy holding up a large fish. "That's me. The feisty thing almost pulled me into the water before I landed him."

Caroline only gave the photo a fleeting glance. Her interest in anything about him and his family was zero.

"That's Delvin. He was two years younger than me." He held the album so Caroline could see.

She stiffened when his studied gaze went from the colored photo of a little boy petting a dog to Danny who was sitting on the floor nearby,

Was he trying to find a family resemblance? Both youngsters had light-brown hair, slightly wavy, a full face and slender bone structure—just like a million other little boys. Caroline wasn't about to sit there looking at his

family album while he searched for family re-
semblances to her son. He must have felt her
withdrawal because he quickly closed the
album and grabbed her hand before she could
get to her feet. "Caroline, you have to know
I'm pulled in two directions on this. Until I
know for sure…"

"Well, that shouldn't take very long." She
jerked her hand away and stood up. "If your
private snoop is any good at all, he'll verify the
adoption papers in quick order. Then we both
can put this little charade of yours behind us."

"Charade?" He stood up and faced her. "Is
that what you think?"

"Don't insult me by pretending your romantic
interest in me has been anything but a calculated
effort to gather information about my son."

Heat flared in his eyes. "You seem to forget
my so-called romantic interest in you was there
before the Jacuzzi discovery."

She answered in the same accusing tone.

"You deliberately turned my feelings into an advantage when you needed more information. And I gave it to you. Now you don't have to pretend anymore. And neither do I!"

Before Wes could reply, Stella came back with Tim and Shane. She sent a questioning look at Wes and Caroline as if puzzled by their stiff postures and facial expressions.

Caroline was relieved when Wes ignored Stella's jibes about not staying to help and quickly disappeared.

DELIO'S CALL came in about four o'clock that afternoon. Wes's hand tightened on the receiver when the detective identified himself.

"I hope you're ready for this, Wes," Delio said in a warning tone.

"I am. What do you have?"

"The papers are fraudulent. Phonies. They're remarkable copies of the necessary legal adoption documents. Interestingly enough, the lawyer's signature appears to be authentic. I've compared the handwriting with other documents of George Goodman, the lawyer who supposedly handled the adoption. He closed up his office about four years ago and apparently left Colorado. I haven't had time to try and track him down."

"You're saying Goodman falsified the adoption records?"

"That's my guess. Thomas and Caroline Fairchild might have been completely unaware that their lawyer was only going through the pretense of a legal adoption." Delio cleared his throat. "I have no proof, Wes. Not yet. Goodman could have been raking in money on illegal adoptions. You know, providing innocent couples with black-market babies for exorbitant fees."

Wes found it hard to breathe. His mind raced with the implications of what Delio was saying. *Fraudulent papers. Black-market babies.*

"We're still a long way from verifying that

the kidnappers of your son were part of this illegal traffic," Delio cautioned. "It's going to take time."

"I want this resolved! Hire all the help you need. Double your own fee."

"That isn't necessary, Wes. Calm down. The little boy is in good hands, isn't he? Just keep on eye on him. Is there a chance the mother would agree to some DNA testing?"

"I doubt it. Her attitude isn't very promising," Wes admitted. "When I tell her about the fraudulent papers, she may cooperate."

"Give it a try. I'll do my best to get a line on George Goodman and any other adoptive parents who might have gone through his office. Maybe I can locate a secretary or another office worker who worked for him and who would be willing to talk."

"Offer them a bribe if you have to," Wes ordered. "And get back to me as soon as you have something."

"Will do," Delio promised and hung up.

As Wes leaned back in his chair, he mentally reviewed their conversation. Every new discovery seemed to validate his belief that Caroline Fairchild's adopted son could be his. Now, he had no choice but to pressure her to cooperate, even though that meant destroying every remaining thread of tender feelings between them.

Chapter Thirteen

After putting Danny to bed, Caroline stood staring out the window, her thoughts as scattered as a startled flock of pigeons. She hugged herself against a deepening chill as Wes's voice kept ringing in her ears.

Until I know for sure...

What more proof did he need? He'd seen the legal papers. His detective would verify them. Then what? Would Wes put all his power, money and influence to discredit her personally? If he failed to get Danny one way, he might try another and continue forever.

When a demanding knock sounded on the

sitting-room door and she saw who it was, she just stood there, blocking the doorway.

"We have to talk."

"What about?" she asked without moving.

Wes scowled. "I don't think we should have this discussion with me standing in the hall."

"I don't think we should be discussing anything at all," she snapped.

"It's very, very important."

She had no choice but to step back and let him into the room. "What, no nightcap this time?" she chided. "Didn't you find out everything you wanted to know the last time?"

He motioned to the couch. "Let's sit down."

She stiffened. Did he really think she going to sit lovingly beside him as she'd done before? The memories of his tender touch and light kiss on her forehead were torture enough. "I prefer to stand."

"Caroline, I think you'd better sit."

"Are you trying to frighten me?"

"I have some important information that you should know about."

"From your detective, no doubt," she replied in a sarcastic tone.

"Yes."

"Well, I guess I'd better hear his excuses for missing the adoption records in the first place." She eased down in a nearby chair.

Sitting on the edge of the couch, he leaned forward and the way he was looking at her brought a sudden tightening to her chest.

"Delio called me and gave me his report."

Her voice was strained. "And—"

"Caroline, there's no easy way to tell you this. He checked Danny's adoption papers. They're fake."

Unexpected laughter was her initial response. What kind of manipulation was this? Did Wes really think she'd believe such a preposterous lie? He must take her for a fool. She wasn't some fluffy-headed woman he could manipulate any way he pleased to get what he wanted.

"How interesting, Wes. And how did your high-paid investigator come to that conclusion?"

"Delio was able to verify that the papers are fraudulent. No legal papers were ever filed. That's the reason Delio couldn't find any official record of Danny's adoption when he searched."

"Really?" she replied in a scathing tone. "And how did you manage to arrange that, Wes? Pay enough people to alter the truth so you could back up this outrageous claim?"

His eyes hardened. "I know this is a shock—"

"The shock is that you would stoop so low. You think your power and money can take away my son because you lost yours!"

His temper flared. "You can't believe that!"

"That's exactly what I believe. And I'll tell you something else. I'll never give Danny up, no matter how you manipulate the truth or how many people you pay to lie!"

"That's enough!" He clenched his jaw and took several deep breaths as if to bring his temper back under control. "There's a way we can settle this quickly, Caroline. Just give your consent for DNA testing."

"And trust you not to manipulate the results?" she replied in a scathing tone. "I was married to a doctor, remember? I know how easily tests can be manipulated and twisted if they fall into the wrong hands. What guarantee do I have that you won't use your money and resources to falsify the results?"

He stared at her. "You can't really believe what you're saying. I only want to know the truth...for all our sakes."

"I know the truth."

"Do you? You told me your husband and his lawyer handled everything. You admitted you never met the woman they said gave the baby up for adoption. How do you know she really existed?"

"Because I have no reason to doubt it. No, I won't consent to the tests. Absolutely not."

"If I present the situation to a judge, I'm sure I can get a court order." He stood up and moved quickly to her chair. "Please, Caroline, don't destroy everything between us." He grabbed her hands and pulled her to her feet. "You have to know how I feel about you."

"I do now," she said, remaining rigid and stiff in his arms. "You played me very well. I never suspected that romancing me was just a means to an end."

"That's not true. I was falling for you even before the question of Danny's parentage arose." He gently eased back a lock of hair drifting down on her forehead. "And you have deep feelings for me, I know you do."

"Wrong again," she lied. "I never took our touch of romance seriously. When Nicole arrived on the scene I was glad I hadn't."

"You were jealous?" His mouth eased into a

faint smile. "For your information I told Nicole how I felt about you. I confessed that at long last I'd found a woman who was everything I wanted. How can we have any kind of a future together until we resolve this? Don't you see, darling, I love you." He brought his mouth closer to hers.

Her senses were suddenly filled with his scent, the warm pull of his body and the caressing sensations of his hands tracing the smallness of her waist and the warm curves of her hips.

"We need to know the truth for both our sakes," he whispered.

The truth!

The word challenged her on every level of her being. She pulled away from him. "I already know the truth. You're willing to lie, cheat and bribe to get what you want."

He looked as if she'd slapped him.

She turned away without saying anything more and as she shut the bedroom door behind her, she leaned back against it and let a flood of hot tears stream down her cheeks.

AFTER A TORTUOUS, sleepless night, Caroline decided that staying at the lodge any longer was out of the question. She had to leave. The decision brought up a myriad of problems that would have to be faced. Somehow, she'd have to cope. No home. No job. No money. At the moment none of the problems were as dire as was remaining under the same roof with a man who had manipulated her feelings and who coveted her son.

She wasn't quite sure how she would explain her sudden departure to Stella, but when she and Danny went down for breakfast she learned Felicia had already told Stella about Wes's interest in Danny.

"I never heard anything so ridiculous," Stella said as she joined Caroline and Danny at their table. "Wes has always brooded about the kidnapping, but I never thought he'd go off the deep end like this."

Caroline shot a meaningful look at Danny. "Let's not talk about this now."

"Oh. Oh, yes," Stella said quickly, getting the silent message. "We'll talk about that later. Anyway, I was wondering what you thought about making some long-distance calls today. We could put in some orders and arrange for workmen to get things started."

Caroline pretended to listen to Stella's monologue, but her stomach muscles were tight and her thoughts heavy with too many unanswered questions. Stella didn't seem to notice.

After breakfast she decided to leave Danny with Felicia for the morning. She didn't want him around when she informed Stella of her decision to leave. Things might get a little heated when she demanded payment for time spent on the project. She didn't kid herself—breaking her contract might mean no money at all.

"Oh, goodie," Cassie said, clapping her hands when she saw Danny. "We'll play racetrack!"

"I want the red car," he quickly declared.

Felicia smiled at Caroline. "Are you feeling more yourself today?"

Caroline wanted to light into her for talking to Stella about Wes and Danny, but with the two children standing there she had to hold her tongue.

"I'll be back to pick him up for lunch," Caroline told Felicia and left.

Stella was already in the workroom and was standing looking out the window when Caroline came in. Heavy clouds hung low and a gray mist was seeping down the mountainside, draining all color from the trees, boulders and remaining patches of snow.

"Looks like another storm brewing," Stella said as she turned around.

Caroline stiffened. She hadn't given any

thought to the weather. Getting snowed in certainly wasn't in her plans. A new sense of urgency sluiced through her.

Stella sat down at the work table and started talking about materials they needed to order before workmen were scheduled to arrive.

Caroline took a deep breath. "I'm sorry to interrupt you, Stella, but we have to talk."

With a questioning frown, Stella put down the catalog she had in her hand.

"I really don't know how to explain all of this," Caroline began and then faltered.

"I'm listening," Stella responded in her businesslike tone, obviously impatient with the delay in carrying out her agenda for the morning.

"I'm glad you know about Wes's fixation on Danny. You'll understand why I can't remain here any longer."

"What are you saying?"

"I'm sorry, Stella, but I've made up my mind. I've decided to leave right away."

Her eyes sparked with disbelief. "No, you can't! We have a contract."

"Yes, I know, but I was hoping you'd understand the situation, Stella, and pay me for time spent." Quickly Caroline began listing the decisions that had been made in the selection of furniture, window dressings and accessories for the main room. She avoided mentioning the remaining areas in the lodge on the redecorating list.

Stella was silent throughout this recitation and Caroline wondered if she had even been listening. She waved a hand in a dismissing gesture when Caroline had finished.

"I don't intend to finish this decorating project alone," she declared.

"You don't understand…" Caroline began.

"Yes, I think I do. Wes has put you in a very uncomfortable position. I certainly don't blame you for wanting to put some distance between the two of you." She paused. "And I think I know how to achieve that."

"How?"

"Wes leaves instead of you." She smiled as if the solution was so simple there was no question about it. "You stay. He goes."

"Are you serious?"

"Wes has overstayed his planned time here, anyway. I'll talk to him. He'll go back to Houston and that will solve everything. You can complete your contract and get paid the generous full amount we agreed upon." She glanced at her watch. "I bet I can catch him in his suite right now."

She was heading for the door before Caroline could tell her about the detective Wes had hired and Delio's false accusations about Danny's adoption.

"Stella, you don't know the whole story," Caroline called after her, but she just gave a wave of her hand and turned down the hall in the direction of Wes's suite.

Caroline rested her head in her hands. She

could imagine the conversation between the two of them. After Stella heard the fabricated story about Danny's adoption, she'd fall in line and support Wes. Family ties were stronger than hired help. Trying to collect any money from either of them was a long shot. It made more sense to get back to Denver and try to line up another decorating contract.

She walked out of the work room and went downstairs to the telephone alcove. Taking a deep breath, she called Betty at the store.

"Things have gotten worse here," Caroline told her. "I plan to leave the lodge very early in the morning. Can we be your house guests again?"

"Of course. Love to have you," Betty responded quickly. "What's going on, Caroline?"

"It's complicated. I'll tell you when I get there." Caroline swallowed hard. "I may need a good lawyer."

"Oh, you've decided to shake up the insurance company? I don't blame you. It's about time they paid up."

"No, it's not about the insurance. It's personal."

"Uh-oh. That sounds ominous."

"It is." After promising to tell her everything when she got to Denver, Caroline hung up.

She sat there staring at the telephone for a long moment. When she heard a muffled breathing nearby, she swung her head around. Dexter was loitering a few feet away.

"Do you make a habit of eavesdropping?" she snapped.

He just smiled as he sauntered over to the telephone desk. "Why do you need a lawyer? You aren't thinking about suing the almighty Wainwright family, are ya? Don't tell me you're going to try to put dear old Wes on the rack?" he chided with an amused curl of his pudgy lips. "Collect for breach of promise or the like? Not that he hasn't been there before. I have to warn you, though. It'll be harder than a steel bullet to collect anything from him. He likes to romance them and leave them."

"And you're telling me all this because…?"

"I've been watching what's going on between you two. I knew Wes was just playing you along. Couldn't figure it out—not that you're not attractive and all that. Just didn't seem his type."

"Well, I guess you were right about that," Caroline said as she stood up. "Now, if you'll excuse me…"

"Are you really taking off in the morning?" His tone was plainly hopeful.

"Yes."

"Then maybe Wes and I can get back to carrying out some of our plans."

"I guess that's up to him," Caroline replied just as bluntly. If she hadn't been caught up in her own emotional whirlwind, she would have realized Dexter was jealous of the time and attention Wes had been giving her. She'd come between two old buddies. No wonder Dexter was glad to see her go.

Clearly she'd made an enemy without even realizing it. Had Dexter been the one to put the children in danger with that treacherous treasure-hunt game? Maybe his jealousy over Wes's time extended to them, too.

She felt Dexter's eyes boring into her back as she went down the hall. Instead of going upstairs, she decided to check out the main room for the last time. Maybe she could take care of one last job before she left in the morning.

The large room was stark and nearly empty. As she moved about, her footsteps echoed on the bare floor and gusts of wind whistled in the dark fireplace. The lonely sounds matched the emptiness she felt inside. She closed her eyes and was visualizing the beautiful room that she would never see when she heard footsteps in the hall.

She stiffened when Wes appeared in the

doorway a moment later. After last night, she was hoping to avoid him altogether.

"Dex told me he thought you came in here," he said and quickly crossed the room to where she stood. "Stella told me you're leaving. If you do that we'll never be able to settle the conflict between us."

"You'd better believe it's already settled," she countered.

"What if I promised to pull Delio off the investigation? Would you stay then?"

"Why on earth would you do that?"

"I can't let it end like this. I've waited too long to find someone like you." He put his hands gently on her shoulders. "And you love me, I know you do."

She ignored the warmth of his nearness and met his gaze squarely. "I'm leaving and there's nothing you can do to stop me."

Deep lines of defeat etched his face. "All right, you win. I'll do what Stella wants. I'll leave. You stay and finish the job. I promise to halt the investigation until we talk again. You have to believe me, I won't do anything that jeopardizes yours and Danny's happiness."

As if to seal his promise, he bent his head and before she could protest his lips captured hers possessively and his quick tongue sent desire racing through her. She was breathless when he pulled back and searched her face.

"You're a better liar than I am if you claim that didn't mean anything."

As he turned away and walked out of the room, she muffled a cry to call him back.

Chapter Fourteen

Caroline didn't see Wes the rest of the day. Stella seemed to think everything had been settled to her satisfaction and didn't make any reference to their talk. Caroline decided Wes must have convinced her that he'd leave so she wouldn't have to.

"Begin checking on businesses we can hire to make basic renovations," she had ordered with her usual briskness when she found Caroline in the main room. "Try the Denver and Colorado Springs directories first, but I doubt we'll have any luck getting them to come this distance. Probably, Grand Junction is our best bet. We have to get them on the job right away."

Caroline nodded. Her decision to leave in the morning had not changed. She'd make a list and leave it for Stella. Even if Wes left, there was no assurance he wouldn't return before her job was completed. Nothing would have changed. Their conflict would be the same.

As soon as she and Danny returned to their rooms after an early dinner, she began packing.

"Whatcha doing?" Danny asked when he saw her putting everything in their suitcases.

"Packing."

"What for?"

"We're driving back to Denver tomorrow."

"Is Cassie going with us?" he asked with eager innocence.

"No, she has to stay here...with her father."

He scowled. "Why can't we stay, too?"

"This isn't our home."

"But we don't got one. It burned down." A worried look crossed his expressive face.

Caroline sat down on the bed and put an arm

around him. "I know, honey. It's going to be all right. We'll stay with Betty and Jim until we get another one."

"I like it better here. Why do we have to go?"

She held him close and rested her chin on top of his head. "It's time."

"Why?"

"Because mommy's job is finished here," she lied. As he snuggled back against her, she whispered. "I love you a whole bunch, my Danny boy. We're going to be just fine. I promise. When we get back to Denver, we can go to the zoo again and see all the new baby animals. You'd like that."

She continued her breezy chatter as she tucked him in bed. "What book would you like me to read tonight?"

"Who Am I?"

For a moment his answer seemed like a question. She stiffened before she realized he was just repeating the title. Would he ask the same question of her someday? The story seemed more poignant than ever.

When he was sound asleep and all the suitcases except one had been packed and closed, she dropped down in a chair and put her face in her hands.

Maybe they wouldn't be safe in Denver!

Fearful thoughts raced through her head. What if Wes convinced the authorities that she was keeping Danny illegally? If his high-priced lawyers successfully proved she was guilty of breaking the law, the authorities could take Danny away from her.

She went over everything that had happened. At first Wes had tried the easy way to get his hands on her son by romancing her. His declarations of love were hollow and had been coldly manipulative under the present circumstances.

Caroline rose to her feet and began restlessly moving around the room. She didn't believe for one minute his promise to halt his investi-

gation. She was positive Delio would stay o
the job, searching for some kind of entrap
ment that would further Wes's determinatio
to claim Danny. She needed to be prepared
But how? Where would she get the money t
hire professional help who could verify th
truth—an unmarried young woman had give
Danny up for adoption. If DNA testing wa
required, she wanted to have a controlle
situation in place where the Wainwrigl
millions couldn't influence the outcome. Sh
knew how easily someone who handled th
testing could manipulate blood samples—
the price was right.

All of these thoughts raced through her hea
with growing intensity. Outside her windov
thickening clouds in the dark sky hid the sta
and moon from view. She could hear a higl
pitched moaning wind whipping through ta
ponderosa pines. No sign of snow yet, than
heavens. If they left the lodge early enough

the morning, they ought to be able to reach the main roads before any potential storm settled in.

She quickly changed into her flannel pajamas and impulsively slipped into bed with Danny. As she nestled close to him, the familiar scent of his soft hair and the warmth of his little body created a rush of emotions that brought tears to her eyes. She clung to a simple truth. *I'm his mother.*

WES WAS STILL awake at midnight when the first icy snowflakes hit the windows. He got out of bed, fixed himself a Scotch and soda and put a couple more logs on the fire. Sleep seemed a long way off.

He kept going over the last scene with Caroline. He'd handled everything wrong. For a fleeting moment, she had responded to his kisses with the same fire and passion but cold rejection had flashed into her eyes as she pulled away.

It was all his fault. A weird set of circum
stances had fired a hope that his son was sti
alive and he'd been so focused on finding out th
truth, he'd failed to be concerned whether o
not Caroline might be threatened by his action
He'd moved too fast. Now he had to find a wa
quickly to repair the damage. Somehow he ha
to gain back her confidence and love.

After a restless night, he was up earl
Without taking time to make his usual pot o
coffee, he hurried downstairs.

During the night, the storm had settled i
Already this second snow of the season wa
piling up drifts as falling flakes whipped acro
the ground. Wes knew that sometimes Octob
storms in Colorado were as fierce as those
midwinter.

Trudie was busy setting up the buffet whe
he came in. She was the only one in the roo
and gave him a look of surprise. "My goodnes
look at you. Up and about this early?"

He glanced at his watch. He'd wanted to make sure he didn't miss Caroline at breakfast. "I guess everybody's sleeping in this morning."

"Nope. Just the opposite," she said, shaking her head. "Usually it's another hour before anyone shows up. Not this morning, though. You just missed having company for breakfast."

"Who?"

"Caroline and her little boy were here first. Then Tim came in and joined them. They just left a few minutes ago." Trudie shook her head. "Tim went to bring her car around front. Can you believe it? She's going to start out in this storm with that little boy."

Wes didn't hear anything else. Trudie was still talking when he bolted out of the room. Racing down the hall to the lodge's main entrance, he threw open the front door and looked outside.

No sign of Caroline's small car.

Maybe they'd gone to the garage with Tim.

Snowflakes instantly coated his hair as h
dashed around the corner of the building. A
five garage doors were closed, but there was
light on in the small office.

Tim was just coming through an inner do
when Wes burst into the room. "Are they st
here?"

"You just missed them. Not more than fi
minutes."

"Why in the hell didn't you stop her?"

"I tried. She's one stubborn woman. I kne
it was a foolhardy thing to do, but I just tal
orders around here, remember? What did yo
want me to do? Hogtie her?"

There was a bitterness in his voice Wes h
not heard before. Tim was always so so
spoken and accommodating, it was easy
overlook his feelings, but Wes didn't have tin
to worry about that now.

"I've got to stop her before she's drivin
blind in the snow, down those hairpin curve

He pushed past Tim and ran to where his Jeep was parked. A glance at the gas gauge told him Dex had not filled the tank after taking Nicole back to Telluride. He swore as he backed out of the garage into a whirl of snow that his windshield wipers failed to completely clear.

CAROLINE HAD SCARCELY made it past the lake and started down the narrow serpentine road when she realized she'd made a terrible mistake. Her hands were rigid on the steering wheel as she hunched over in her seat. Whipping snow assaulted her headlights and blew blinding snowflakes against the windshield. She had only a small area of visibility as the wipers pushed the snow aside.

Forced to drive at a snail's pace, Caroline realized that her plan to make it to the main highway before the storm worsened was going to be impossible. Trees and rocks on the hillsides were already masked by layers of thickening white and snow on the road was building up at an unbelievable rate. She had no choice but to turn around and go back to the lodge.

Turn around where?

The narrow road was cupped on both sides by vaulting rock cliffs or thick stands of evergreens. She could barely make out the edges of the pavement. The wind quickened with every passing minute, sending more snow whipping across the road and obscuring her vision.

"I don't like it," Danny said, sitting in his car seat behind her.

"We'll turn around and go back," she told him with false calmness.

"Right now?"

"As soon as there's a wide spot in the road."

She hoped there would be a pull-out space ahead every time the car navigated a serpentine curve. Even though she couldn't remember any, surely the road had to widen enough for a turn-around before long.

She fought the mesmerizing effect of snow-flakes swirling into the feeble radius of her headlights.

And then it happened!

Even at a snail's pace, she lost control without warning. The car hit a slick patch of ice! In a split second, it left the pavement and went over the side of the mountain road.

Careening downward, the small car was caught in a slight trough where a natural runoff of water from above had frozen and created an icy chute down the hillside into a mountain stream below.

BEHIND THE WHEEL of the Jeep, Wes maintained a speed that drew on his familiarity with the roads. Wes had driven here often enough to have memorized every twist and turn. He hoped with every curve to see Caroline's car just ahead. If she was driving with any caution, she couldn't have gotten very far. He knew the storm was settling in with a vengeance. She had no business trying to drive anywhere in this weather, especially in that car of hers!

He was rehearsing a good bawling out in his mind when he glimpsed her taillights just going around a curve ahead. Good. He'd make her pull over and get herself and Danny into his car. There was an old forestry road for a turn around about five miles ahead.

He came around the curve and was about to put a hand on his horn to alert her when her taillights suddenly disappeared.

What in the—

Leaning forward he strained to see ahead. He would have passed the place where her car had plunged off the road if fresh tire tracks in the snow had not indicated the spot. In a matter of minutes, the tracks would have been filled with snow and he would have missed them.

He braked and leaped out of the Jeep. As fast as his boots could cover the ground, he rushed to the side of the road. Shielding his eyes from the snow, he searched the snowy terrain below.

There was no sign of the car in the smooth whiteness of rocks and trees. He focused on the tire tracks that plunged downward out of sight and saw they stayed in a kind of ravine made by years of water runoff from above.

The car could have slid all the way down.

Wes knew that if by some miracle a car reached the bottom of the steep mountain slope without being smashed, it would be engulfed in the paralyzing cold water of a mountain stream.

Panic sent him scrambling downward at a dangerous speed as he bounded over snow-covered boulders, through trees heavy with white branches and down steep, slippery banks.

The pain in his chest from the cold, thin air grew with every breath. He knew at this high altitude hypothermia was a real threat.

His worst fear was realized when he broke out of the trees and saw the car half-buried in the stream. It was wedged in between large boulders that had fallen from the slopes above. The front of the car was nose-down in the water not very far from the bank. The back half of the car was in the air with its rear wheels raised and dangling.

As Wes splashed his way into the snowy stream, layers of thin ice broke under his boots. His legs were numb in the few seconds it took to reach the car. Since the front windows were submerged, he scrambled up on a slippery rock to reach a back door which was half raised out of the water.

"Caroline! Danny!"

The cold air made his voice thick and muffled. He jerked with all his might to try and open the door but the rock on which he knelt held it firm.

He couldn't hear anything inside.

If Caroline was unconscious in her seat belt, she'd be underwater.

Only a small portion of a rear window was free of the large boulder and clear enough to see through. Frantically, he rubbed the window with his jacket sleeve to try and clear it. He thought he could see the top of Danny's head but he wasn't sure.

"Danny! Caroline!"

He made a move to go around to the other side of the car. Maybe that door and window weren't blocked by rocks. When he heard a faint noise, he froze. Was it only the sound of moving water fooling him?

"Wes…"

This time there was no mistake.

"Yes, yes," he shouted. "I'm here!"

When she pressed her face against the tiny area of the window he could see, an unbelievable relief washed over him. Her hair was drenched, blood coated a small cut on her forehead and her eyes were glazed.

She was alive! For a few seconds he couldn't

think beyond that miracle. She must have scrambled into the back when the front of the car filled with water. His heart leaped in thankfulness a second later when her face disappeared and Danny pressed his against the windowpane.

The little boy's tearful eyes widened when he saw Wes and he put his little hand against the window in a wordless plea.

"Yes, I'll get you out. Just hold on! I'll check the other side."

Quickly, he let himself down into the stream again and waded around the car. The granite boulders wedged against the other door were just as heavy and immoveable. Once again he was unable to shift them enough to allow passage even if they broke the windows as a means of escape.

Only one other window remained free of rocks and water.

Wes climbed around to the back and studied

the car's narrow rear window. It was the only possible exit free of rock and water. Standing on built-up slabs of rocks that had tumbled from the hillside above, he would be able to break the glass and help them through the cleared window frame.

Danny would be able to slither through, but a grown woman?

When he brushed away the layer of snow on the narrow window, he could see them huddled together.

"I'm going to break the window," he yelled. "Turn away." His fingers were numb under his gloves as he grasped a wet stone and shattered the window glass. When he'd cleared the frame of jagged shards, he looked through the opening. Half the interior of the car was submerged in water. Caroline had her arm around Danny as they cowered on some piled-up suitcases.

"Okay, let's go!"

Quickly, Caroline helped Danny up to the

window. Wes took hold of him from the other side and guided him through. Then he turned and set the boy down on the closest snowy boulder.

"Stay there until I get your mother."

"I'm…cold…" The child looked like an abandoned waif hunched there. Fortunately Caroline had put him in his snowsuit for the trip.

When Wes quickly turned back to the window, he saw that Caroline was already halfway out. Thank heavens for her slim and supple figure, he thought as he helped maneuver her through the narrow opening. She was coming out head-first and he pulled her into his arms as the rest of her body dropped free of the window frame.

They clung together with a fierceness that defied any words. Caroline's tears and blood smeared his face as his numbed hands and soaked gloves held her firmly against him. There was only time for a brief moment of thankfulness. Danger still lay in a growing storm that could claim them before they reached the road.

Shivering, lungs hurting and limbs turning blue, they started the strenuous climb upward. Would they be able to make it up to the warmth of the Jeep before they were all overcome with frozen limbs?

Wesley ended up carrying Danny on his back. Caroline valiantly tried to keep up but fell repeatedly to her knees.

Several times, Wes railed at her when she crumpled and seemed ready to give up. "Move! On your feet. Now!"

He knew what torture she was going through. The temperature of his body had fallen to dangerous levels and he could feel his heart and lungs beginning to protest.

Every time he squinted upward, he thought the rim of the hill was receding farther and farther into the distance. His eyes began playing tricks on him when he saw two head-lights shining down on them.

Then he heard a shout. His eyelashes were so heavy with snow, he could barely see a dark figure moving down the slope toward them.

"Hold on. I'm coming!"

Wes recognized Tim's voice even before the big man was close enough to see. Never in his life had Wes felt such total relief. With Tim helping Caroline, Wes's strength seemed to be renewed and the burden of carrying Danny seemed easier.

They were closer to the road than Wes had realized. In a matter of a few minutes they were in the warmth of the SUV.

They used everything they could find in the SUV to wrap around themselves—hunting jackets, lap robes and seat blankets. All three of them were suffering from hypothermia.

Danny whimpered as Caroline held him close. Shivering in her arms, his little face was drained of color. Her voice was weak and strained as she tried to soothe him.

"I'm getting you all to the Alpine Medical Center," Tim said in a tone that told Wes he was no longer in charge. "Dr. Boyd needs to have a look at you,"

Wes couldn't have argued if he'd wanted to. His body was floating away in numbness which had sapped his muscular strength and was threatening to make him helpless against an invading drowsiness.

Chapter Fifteen

Wes knew Dr. William Boyd personally. H
was a handsome man in his early fifties wh
could have been chosen for the cover of
Colorado outdoor magazine. His rugge
build and a complexion weathered by su
and snow betrayed his love of climbin
fishing and skiing.

He'd been a guest at the lodge several time
and when Wes was brought into emergency o
a gurney, he took a double look as if h
couldn't believe his eyes.

"Wes! What in blazes happened to you?"

"I…I went swimming…in a creek," h
croaked. "Look after the others. I'm… fine."

"The hell you are. We'll have a look at all of you…now!" He nodded to his staff.

Caroline and Danny disappeared and a couple of nurses took charge of Wes. One stuck a thermometer in his mouth, the other one began stripping off the wet clothes.

After wrapping his chilled body in an electric blanket, they warmed his feet and gave him a mug of tea to drink.

"Your core temperature is only ninety degrees," Dr. Boyd told him when he returned a few minutes later. "You're damn lucky you all got here when you did."

"What about Caroline and Danny?" Wes asked anxiously.

"They're better off than you are. I hear you're some kind of hero. Jumping into a frozen stream, breaking glass to get them out." He winked at Wes. "Of course, you've always been a fool for a pretty lady."

"This one's special."

"Oh, it's like that, is it? Well, glad to hear i Time you settled down."

"Yes," Wes agreed.

"She was lucky that her car took a nose-div into the soft bottom of the creek instead c plowing into something solid. Fortunately he airbag protected her enough that she coul climb into the back seat for the boy. Neither c them suffered anything more than a fev bruises and scratches."

"Thank God." Wes breathed.

"The little boy's a sharp one." The docto smiled. "The nurse offered him some warr tea and he asked very politely, 'Haven't yo got any hot chocolate?'"

"He's quite a boy," Wes agreed, no wanting to think how close they'd come t losing him.

"The good news is the three of you ought t be able to leave emergency later today. I don see any evidence of lingering frostbite. Onc we get the core temperatures stabilized we'll release all of you."

What would Caroline do now? Go back to the lodge or find other transportation to Denver?

"All of you need to stay warm, though," the doctor added. "Because of lingering fatigue I suggest all of you spend the night in Telluride. The weathermen are saying it's going to snow the rest of the day but will move on sometime before tomorrow morning."

Wes nodded. He wasn't about to make the trip back to the lodge. "I'll need to talk with Tim."

"The poor guy has been pacing the floor. I'll tell him you want to see him."

When Tim came in a few minutes later, he looked worried and asked anxiously, "How you doing?"

"Good. Caroline and Danny, too. The doctor's going to release us this afternoon."

"Great." He let out a breath he'd obviously been holding. "You guys had me scared. I called Stella and told her what had happened. Boy, was she surprised! She didn't even know Caroline had left the lodge. She really ripped into me like you did for not stopping them." He shook his head. "I'm sorry, I guess I really dropped the ball on that one."

"This isn't your fault, Tim," Wes assured him. "Thank you for coming after us the way you did. And I shouldn't have yelled at you. Anyway, it's over and done with. Contact the Stonehaven Hotel and make reservations for all of us tonight. Oh, yes, and telephone the lodge and have Dexter and one of the men take the Jeep back to the lodge before the storm gets any worse."

"Stella will want to know if we're coming back tomorrow."

Wes took a deep breath. "I'm not sure." He didn't want to tell Tim that everything depended upon what Caroline decided to do. She might insist on him taking her to Denver.

as she'd planned. At the moment, he only knew he would make whatever concessions he had to in order to mend the situation between them. He'd pushed her too hard, too fast.

WHEN DR. BOYD told Caroline he was dismissing the three of them later in the day, she was surprised and relieved. Danny had bounced back without any problem. Once they'd moved him into the same room with her and once she knew her son was all right, her concern had centered on Wes.

"Wes is okay then?" she anxiously asked the doctor. She'd been terribly worried about him. By the time Tim had driven them into Telluride, Wes's face had been void of color, his mouth had an unhealthy blue tinge and his eyes wavered with an unfocused gaze.

"Yes, he's fine, but another couple of hours could have made a serious difference. He's one brave man." He eyed her as if he was about to say something more, but just gave her a smile as he left the room.

Caroline couldn't believe how Wes had totally ignored his own safety to rescue them. It touched her deeply the way he'd plunged down the steep mountainside and waded in icy water and blowing snow to get them out of the car. She'd never forget the way he struggled back up the rugged slope with Danny on his shoulders. Just thinking about his selfless action brought tears to her eyes.

"Why are you crying, Mama?"

She swallowed hard. "Because I'm grateful...for everything."

"I don't like it here."

"I don't either but the doctor says we can go soon."

"Back to Cassie's house?" Danny asked hopefully.

"I...I don't think so."

"Where?"

She was searching for an answer when Wes walked into the room. Obviously he'd over-heard Danny's question. "How about a nice hotel with a warm swimming pool?"

"Goody! Can we, Mom?" Danny begged.

With both of them waiting hopefully, and knowing she needed time to sort things out, there was only one answer she could give.

THEY LEFT the medical center about three o'clock in the afternoon. Tim drove them to the fashionable Stonehaven Hotel. Built of pink stone, an old-world charm was evident in the building's irregular roof line, wooden balco-nies and large recessed windows. Wes had stayed there many times before and when they registered, he was assured that his usual suite of rooms was available and ready.

Since Tim had friends in the area, he declined Wes's offer of a hotel room. "I'll check with you first thing in the morning," he told him.

"You'll probably have made some decisions b
then. I promised to call Stella as soon as I know
anything. I bet she'd be here in a flash if th
weather were decent."

Caroline ignored the questioning look Tin
sent her. No doubt, Stella was having a fit abou
her quitting so abruptly. Handling the presen
was all she could manage at the moment
They'd lost everything in the half-submerged
car. She'd escaped with nothing—not even he
purse or the metal box with the records.

The hospital had dried their clothes so the
had something to wear immediately. She knew
it would take time to get her credit cards reissued
and alert her car insurance. All these detail
seemed rather insignificant when compared to
the wonder that they had escaped with their lives

She had exchanged only a few words with
Wes on the way to the hotel and had even less
to say to him when they entered the luxurious
lobby with its high ceiling, leather carved

chairs and sofas. There was a European elegance about the decor which pleased Caroline and she silently complimented the interior decorator who had achieved such a look of wealth and grace.

A mirror-walled elevator sped them upward to a tastefully decorated suite of rooms with its own balcony and stone fireplace. A luxurious sitting room, marble bathroom and exquisite bedrooms resembled pictures Caroline had seen of Old World luxury hotels.

Even at her best, she would have felt terribly out of place. Trying to cope under the circumstances left her drained. Danny, on the other hand, bounced in and out of the elegant rooms with bubbling curiosity.

"Why don't you and Danny take this room." Wes motioned to a spacious bedroom which was definitely feminine in a mauve-and-pale-green decor. "I usually have the one on the other side of the living room."

And this one is reserved for your lady friends?

Ridiculous tears threatened to fill her eyes as she turned away quickly. "I think I'll have a warm bath and rest."

"Good idea."

"I want to go swimming," Danny said as if he had a vote.

"Maybe later. You and I are going shopping while your mother rests," Wes told him. "I bet there's a toy or two in the gift shop you might like."

"What about Cassie? Can I get her one?"

"We'll see," Wes said as his eyes met Caroline's.

She ignored the questioning lift of one of his eyebrows. Emotionally and physically she wasn't ready to make any firm decisions about what was going to happen next. There were still too many things unresolved between them.

Danny's eyes were dancing with excitement

She suspected Wes was going to have a hard time refusing him anything.

She gave him a hug. "You behave."

He nodded and bounced over to the door.

"You get some rest," Wes told Caroline as he put his arm around her.

She nodded and relaxed in his comforting embrace for a long moment. All of her defenses were down. She needed time to sort out all the emotions that were still reeling like a whirlwind within her.

"Come on!" Danny urged impatiently.

"Okay, buckaroo." He kissed Caroline lightly on the forehead.

She heard her son's excited chatter as they closed the door and made their way down the hall. A delayed reaction from the death-defying experience seemed to hit her all at once. After quickly taking a warm shower, she put on a terry-cloth bathrobe provided as a courtesy of the hotel and slipped into the double, deluxe bed with its heavenly comfort. As the warmth and soft bedding enveloped her like a cocoon, her tight muscles began to relax.

She must have fallen into a deep sleep when the nightmare began. A prodding voice in her subconscious kept telling her to wake up. But she couldn't.

I have to find Danny! Wes never brought him back! The suite was a jumble of doors as she ran through the rooms, searching. As she bounded out into the hall in her bathrobe, a myriad of stairs went everywhere. She kept climbing them, shouting, "He stole my son! He stole my son!"

When she jerked awake, her heart was pounding. Filled with lingering panic, she jumped out of the bed and flung open the door to the living room.

Empty. The only sound was the peppering of icy snow against the windows. A wall clock told her they'd been gone over two hours. She had to find them! She dashed into the bedroom where she'd left her clothes and was just pulling on her boots when she heard a commotion at the hall door.

She dashed out into the living room and as the door opened, an entourage of hotel people came in carrying all kinds of boxes, packages and various pieces of luggage.

As Danny bounded in carrying two sacks, he squealed, "Surprise! Surprise! See what we bought! Lots of stuff. For me and you and Wes!"

Caroline just stood there, unable to find her voice.

"Just pile everything on the chairs and sofas," Wes told the two young women as he set down his own packages on a nearby table. They gave Caroline an envious glance as they put down at least a dozen various-sized bags and boxes labeled Modern Boutique.

An older man smiled at Caroline as he put down the luggage. "I think that's everything."

Wes took some bills out of his wallet for tips and thanked them all. After they left, he walked over to Caroline and took her hand. "You can fill in with other things I missed, but I think this should tide you over."

She blinked as tears tricked down her cheeks and she struggled to get control of her emotions.

"Are you all right? What's the matter? Do you need to go back to the clinic?" He moved quickly to her side. As he put his arm around her, she leaned into the warmth of his embrace. "I shouldn't have left you."

"No, I'm all right," she assured him. "I...I just had a bad dream."

"And no wonder. Any other woman would have been a basket case." He lightly traced her cheek with his fingertip. For a long moment their gaze held in a wordless connection that made his voice husky. "What do you say I fix us both a drink to celebrate?"

She nodded.

While he went to the small bar and fixed a couple of highballs, Caroline looked at Danny's new toys as he played on the floor in front of the sofa.

Wes sat down beside her and put an arm around her shoulder. "I ordered dinner from the Sea and Steak Restaurant downstairs. I didn't think you'd want to go out. Maybe we can come back another time and enjoy Telluride's charm." He searched her face. "Is there going to be another time?"

A brisk knock on the door kept her from giving an uncertain answer to the question.

Danny dominated the conversation while they ate and Caroline was glad when he began to rub his sleepy eyes.

"It's time for bed," she said firmly. "Tell Wes goodnight."

"Can we go swimming tomorrow?"

"Maybe. We'll see."

"Okay." Caroline was surprised when Danny

gave him a peck on the cheek and said "Thanks for getting us out of the car."

After tucking Danny into bed and waiting few minutes until he fell asleep, she returned to the living room. All during the meal, she had been aware of Wes's causal touch and a sexual awareness vibrating between them.

She walked over to where he stood in front of a picture window and for a long moment they stood side by side, looking out at the silvery-white landscape and majestic peaks etched against the night sky.

"Beautiful," she said with a catch in her throat.

"Do you have any idea how close I came to losing you today?" he said in a hoarse voice. "And it would have been my fault."

"No," she protested as she turned toward him.

"Yes, it's the truth. My obsession drove you away. I could have lost you both. Please forgive me." He tipped her chin and looked straight into her eyes. "I'll settle for any part of you life you're willing to share with me. I'll do whatever you say. Be whoever you want me to be. Just don't cut me off from you or Danny."

"I couldn't do that. Not now."

"I love you," he whispered. "Please let me take care of you."

All of her built-up resistance melted away as he kissed her with a hunger that matched her own.

As they lay together, his slow, deep kisses sent a heady supply of desire flowing through her. She delighted in the brush of his chest against her breasts and the caressing touch of his fingers. As his hands molded the curve of her thighs, drawing her beneath him, her surrender seemed brand new. Never had she given herself so completely.

The endearments he whispered as he made love to her mended her shattered emotions. She felt whole, complete.

When he slipped away from her, she lay in

the circle of his arms, fulfilled and renewed. With a deep sigh, she closed her eyes, curled against him and fell into a deep sleep.

Chapter Sixteen

A bright sun was streaming through the window when Caroline awoke. For a moment she was disoriented.

Strange room. Strange bed.

Then she remembered!

Quickly she turned on her side. No Wes. Only a telltale dent in his pillow remained. A moment later, she heard a murmur of voices and Danny's high-pitched laughter in the living room.

Glancing at her watch, she was startled to see how late it was. Her clothes were still in a heap where she'd dropped them, but an inviting erry-cloth robe lay across a nearby chair.

She smiled as she slipped out of bed and put

it on. Wes's thoughtfulness stirred her in strange way. She wasn't used to being care for in such a fashion.

She was totally surprised when she opened th bedroom door and saw that Danny was alread dressed in one of his new outfits. Apparentl Wes had taken care of him while she slept in.

Room service had brought up a breakfas cart and Wes was wiping a chocolate-mil mustache off Danny's mouth as they sat on th sofa. She felt a little self-conscious as sh smiled at them and said, "Good morning."

"You're a sleepyhead!" Danny teased.

"But a beautiful one," Wes added as h quickly stood up and embraced her. "How ar you, sweetheart?"

His remembered touch instantly sparked spiral of unexpected desire in her, and his eye twinkled as if he knew exactly what his caress ing hands were doing to her as they slowl traced the curve of her back.

She felt herself blushing as she drew away. "I think I'm ready for some coffee."

"Wes says we can go swimming this morning," Danny informed her.

"If it's all right with your mother," Wes quickly corrected.

"We'll see," she said in true mother fashion.

After he'd poured her a cup of coffee and offered her several choices from the room-service cart, he commented, "The weather report is good. Everything will start moderating this morning and by afternoon the roads should have been plowed." He searched her face. "We could start back to the lodge right after lunch. If you…"

She knew he was asking if she was going back with him. The question was hardly relevant under the circumstances. She loved him. He knew it.

"Maybe we ought to stop at the clinic before we leave Telluride," she suggested quietly.

An alarmed expression instantly crossed his face. "Is something wrong?"

"I don't know. That's what we need to find out. I think we should consult Dr. Boyd about those blood tests you've been wanting."

His reaction was not at all what she had expected. If anything, he seemed ready to reject her offer. He glanced at Danny and then back at her. "Maybe we should just let things be for the moment."

She knew then he was afraid to know the truth. "I don't think that's a good idea," she said quickly. "The question will always be between us."

She knew their future relationship would be threatened by this fixation of his. When the tests proved a negative match—and she was positive they would—she had to know whether or not he would reject the happiness the three of them had found together.

After a long silence, he nodded. "All right. I'll call Dr. Boyd and set up an appointment for this afternoon. Then we'll head back to the lodge."

"Whoopee!" Danny exclaimed. "Wait 'til I show Cassie all my stuff." His smile faded as he told Wes, "She'll be mad if we don't bring her something."

"Do you think so?" he asked solemnly.

"I bet she'd like one of those Indian dolls we saw."

"All right, we'll buy her one. I think Cassie's found someone to look after her." Wes said as he leaned over and kissed Caroline. "Just the way we're all going to look after each other."

She could tell he was relieved that she'd given in to the DNA testing. Obviously, he was trying to prepare her for the shock that Danny wasn't legally hers, but she was still convinced he was the one heading for an emotional disappointment.

WHILE WES spent time with Danny in the swimming pool, Caroline packed everything in the new luggage. They left the hotel right after lunch and drove to the medical center.

Caroline wasn't sure how to explain to Danny what was going to happen. She guessed they would take a vial of blood the way they did for other tests.

"I'll go first," Wes volunteered. "It's a piece of cake."

Danny frowned. "They give you cake?"

"I'm sure we can find some when we're through," Wes assured him.

"I want chocolate."

"Okay, chocolate, it is."

Caroline smothered a chuckle as she took his hand and the three of them walked into the clinic. The whole procedure took less than fifteen minutes and the nurse didn't draw any blood after all.

"We just do a buccal swab for DNA," the nurse explained.

"What is that?" Caroline asked.

"We just swab the inside of the cheek. And that's that."

"We'll express the samples to a reference laboratory in Denver. It usually takes about a week to get the results."

"That long?" Wes protested. "Isn't there any way to hurry them up?"

"'Fraid not. In fact, if the lab is backed up, it might even be a few days longer," he warned Wes.

Caroline slipped her hand into his. "It's okay. We can wait." She could tell he was anxious.

"Yes, I guess we can," he agreed, smiling. "Let's head for the cafeteria and get Danny that big piece of cake."

As Wes drove the SUV back to the lodge, he could tell that a snowplow had cleared the road that morning. He was glad he had a contact with a firm in Telluride to keep the lodge road plowed when a storm deposited more than four inches of snow. He made arrangements for a tow truck to use a road near the bottom of the creek and pull out Caroline's car.

Caroline sat closely beside him in the passenger seat and Tim was in the back with Danny. When they reached the place in the road where he'd left the Jeep, there was no sign of it. Someone must have returned it to the lodge as he had ordered.

He was aware of Caroline's tension as she sat stiffly beside him, seemingly looking for some clue to where her car had gone over the edge.

"We already passed it," he finally told her gently.

"And if you hadn't been right behind us—"

"But I was," he interrupted quickly. "And you're both here safe and sound. That's all that matters."

She nodded, but her face was still bleached of color and he knew she was reliving that perilous drop down the mountainside and into the water. The horrifying drama would live with both of them forever.

An early-afternoon sun touched the ice-covered lake with a reflected brilliance as they passed it. When they reached the lodge, Wes had barely braked the car when the front door flew open and Stella came rushing out.

Tim chuckled as he admitted, "I called her just before we left the clinic. I'll bet you anything, she's been staring out a front window for God knows how long."

Even before Caroline had her door open, Stella was at the window, smiling at her. The woman's relief was so obvious, Caroline felt a pang of guilt. She'd always prided herself on going the extra mile to make sure she gave a hundred percent of time and effort to any commitment. She wasn't used to letting people down. And running off like that had not been fair to Stella.

As Caroline stepped out of the car, Stella eyed the new burgundy suede slacks and jacket Wes had bought for her. "Wow, that's some outfit. You've been shopping?"

"Wes bought a bunch of stuff," Danny bragged. "Boxes and boxes. And we got a doll for Cassie, too."

"I'm glad everything turned out okay. When Tim told me what had happened, my blood turned cold. I'm glad Wes came to the rescue." She glanced from Caroline to Wes as if she were trying to figure out exactly what had happened between them.

She had her answer when Wes turned to Tim. "Will you take all the luggage up to my suite? They'll be staying with me."

Tim nodded as if the instructions came as no surprise. He smiled, picked up the two new pieces of luggage and disappeared.

Caroline was surprised to see Trudie wiping her hands on her apron as she hurried to greet them when they entered the main room of the lodge.

"Glory be!" she exclaimed, giving Caroline a hug. "When we heard what had happened, I felt horribly responsible. I should have stopped you from going out that door in such weather. Are you and the boy all right?"

Stella spoke up briskly before Caroline could. "They're fine! Can't you see that, Trudie?" As Stella's knowing smile swept from Wes to Caroline, she added, "In fact, I'd say things are very much all right."

Trudie obviously didn't get the veiled implication. Her mind ran on a different track. "Have you had lunch? I can set out something—"

"No need, Trudie, thank you," Wes responded. "We ate before we left the hotel. Maybe we'll like some refreshment later in the afternoon."

"I want to go see Cassie," Danny declared holding up the doll box he'd taken from the car.

"First, we'll get settled," Caroline said firmly.

Danny gave her his lower-lip pout as they made their way upstairs.

Tim had unlocked the suite door with his house key and left the luggage inside. Caroline decided he must have taken one of the back stairways down to his office and made a mental note to thank Tim for all his help.

"What room would you like, Danny?" Wes asked. "When Cassie stays with me, she picks the bedroom closest to the kitchenette." He lowered his voice to a confidential whisper. "I think Cassie gets up in the night and raids the cookie jar."

Danny's eyes lit up. "I'll take that room."

"Smart boy." Wes winked at him and left him in the room looking over some of Cassie's collected toys.

Caroline followed Wes into his bedroom. After putting down the luggage, he turned to her and quickly drew her into his arms as if he'd been too long without the feel of her body cupped against his. His kisses matched a hunger of her own. His murmured endearments ignited a flame of desire between them. With obvious reluctance, he sighed as he slowly set her away from him. If they'd been alone, she knew they would have ended up in bed, but there was Danny.

As if to punctuate his presence, the small boy bounded into the room and plopped himself in the middle of Wes's king-sized bed.

"Why do you need such a big bed?" Danny asked with innocent curiosity. The question was obviously one that Wes was not prepared to answer and Caroline smiled as he deftly sidestepped it.

"Would you like to take that doll to Cassie now?" Wes asked. "I want to let her know I'm back. You could even stay and play with her if it's all right with your mother," he added in all innocence.

"It's all right with his mother," Caroline replied with a knowing smile.

CASSIE MADE a big fuss when she saw Wes and he picked her up in his arms and swung her around. "See who I brought back?" he said as he set her down. He knew his daughter well enough to add, "Danny brought you a present."

"Isn't that nice?" Felicia said in a prompting tone as if she was afraid Cassie was going to forget her manners.

"What is it?" the little girl demanded suspiciously.

"Something you want," Danny said, firmly holding on to the box.

"How do you know?"

"'Cause you said so once." Slowly, he held out the box but made Cassie walk over to him to take it.

Wes smiled. *Good, Danny. You're a smart boy.*

Cassie's squeal of delight when she saw the Indian doll brought a big smile to Danny's face as he said, "Told you so!"

Wes ignored Felicia's questions about Caroline and Danny's return to the lodge. "For the moment, everything will go on as before," he told her.

Her dark eyes seemed to narrow as if she was well aware he wasn't speaking the truth. "I sense big changes. Not good! Not good at all."

Ignoring her doomsday predictions, he promised to pick up the kids later for afternoon refreshments and quickly took his leave.

Returning to the suite, he found Caroline lounging on the bed with the soft coverlet barely covering her nakedness. He quickly joined her and drew her to him with the sure touch of a lover. The zenith of passion and desire they had known the night before flared between them as they made love.

Caroline had fallen asleep in the curve of his arm when he heard the insistent ring of his private phone. He debated answering it, but he remembered that Delio had promised a report Wes wanted to advise him that DNA testing was under way.

Wes gently eased out of bed, pulled on hi shorts and hurried to his office.

The private detective's voice was thick with excitement. "I succeeded in contacting the ex wife of George Goodman, the lawyer who sup posedly handled the Fairchild adoption."

"Good work!"

"She told me he'd skipped to Mexico a few years ago after their divorce. When I men tioned I was representing a family involved in a questionable adoption, she really let loose." He paused. "Wes, you're not going to believe this but it's the God's truth. She swears that in the midst of one of their drunken quarrels, he no-good husband admitted he'd placed a black market baby from a rich family for adoption. He bragged that a woman in the family had paid to have a boy twin kidnapped so that her own son wouldn't lose his position in the male line and lose the entitled inheritance. I thought you should know—"

Wesley slammed down the receiver. "Good God!"

"What is it, Wes?" Caroline stood in the bedroom doorway, putting on her robe.

"Stella! I'll kill her with my bare hands!" He told Caroline what Delio had learned. After quickly dressing, they began searching the lodge with the urgency of a ticking bomb. Stella wasn't in any of her usual places.

"We'll have to tell Felicia to keep a close eye on Danny until we locate her," Caroline said anxiously, and as they hurried to Felicia's apartment, she debated whether or not she should stay close to Danny and let Wes confront Stella.

The decision was taken out of her hands when they found Felicia alone in her apartment. No children were in sight.

"Where are they?" Caroline and Wes demanded almost in unison.

Looking puzzled, Felicia slowly put down her knitting. "Stella came by for them. I thought it would be all right. She took them ice skating on the lake."

"Ice skating!" Wes bellowed in fury. "My God, the lake isn't frozen hard this early in the winter!"

Caroline was close behind him as they raced through the lodge and bounded out the front door.

Their worst fears were realized. Below, on the lake, they could see two small figures moving clumsily a dangerous distance away from the bank. Caroline knew her son could barely maintain his balance on skates. Danny had only been skating a couple of times on a little ice-skating pond that one of the Denver malls maintained for children in the winter.

She shouted his name as they raced down the snowy slope but her voice was driven back into her throat.

Stella was standing on the bank, her hands in her pockets, watching the two clumsy skaters.

Caroline and Wes rushed past her to the edge of the lake.

"Cassie, stop!"

"Danny, come back!"

Caroline kept shouting as Wes moved out gingerly on the thin ice toward them. Both of the children turned around, but it was almost too late. With a warning crack the ice fell away behind them as they slowly started skating toward the bank. Caroline watched with excruciating terror as more and more ice sank into the water.

All three of them might have gone under in the rippling effect of sinking ice if thicker layers of ice spanning out from the edge of the lake hadn't allowed Wes to reach them.

Grabbing a small hand in each of his own, he herded them safely back to the bank.

"Get them to the lodge," he yelled at Caroline as he turned toward Stella with wild fury.

"S-sorry," she stammered as she backed up. "I didn't know that the ice was thin."

"Liar!" He grabbed her. "You're going to tell the truth if I have to choke it out of you."

CAROLINE WAITED restlessly with the children in the suite for Wes's return. Her emotions were racing at such a pace she couldn't process anything in a calm, rational manner. Everything had happened too fast.

She couldn't see anything from the windows to know what was going on because the view was obscured by tall, snow-laden ponderosa pines that brushed against the side of the lodge.

Fortunately Danny and Cassie seemed unaware of the drama unfolding around them. They didn't realize how close they'd come to losing their lives. As they sat on the floor playing a Sesame Street game, they laughed and quarreled with childish innocence.

Caroline was still struggling to absorb the traumatic upheaval of the last few hours when Wes returned to the suite nearly three hours later. She'd managed to settle Danny and Cassie down for a nap and was pacing the floor as her mind raced with unanswered questions.

As he came in, he held out his arms and she went into them with a grateful sigh.

"It's all right," he said wearily as tension underlined his voice. "An FBI agent from Durango took her into custody."

As they sat down on the sofa together, he told her that Stella had admitted everything. "She arranged the kidnapping because she was afraid Shane would lose his inheritance as the next male heir specified in the Wainwright inheritance entitlement. She hired a lover, one of the ranchhands, to kidnap my infant son. Apparently, Stella thought that he'd killed the baby until a couple of months ago."

"How did she find out he hadn't?"

"Because the bastard found out he was dying of cancer and admitted to her on his deathbed that he'd sold the baby to a Colorado lawyer, George Goodman, who handled the adoption of black-market babies. He also told her that a couple named Fairchild had paid big money for the adoption."

Caroline was stunned. How could something that had seemed so right—have been so wrong?

"Stella came to Denver, deciding to check the story out. When she was convinced that Caroline Fairchild was the adoptive mother and Danny Fairchild was my legal heir, she planned to finish the job herself."

Caroline stiffened.

"She set fire to your house, intending that neither one of you would survive. And when you did, she decided to hire you to redecorate the lodge and wait for an opportunity to arrange a fatal accident."

Caroline's eyes widened. "She drew the treasure map!"

His jaw tightened as he nodded. "Sending the kids up that treacherous mountain path to the cabin might have easily resulted in a fatal fall or given her the chance to arrange an accident at the cabin before we found out where they were. She hadn't planned on them showing the map to Shane."

Caroline whispered in a strained voice, "Then Danny's been in danger every minute we've been here!"

Wes tightened his arm around her shoulder. "Apparently, I was paying the two of you too much attention to give her the opportunity she needed. I thwarted her plans without even knowing it. When we returned today and Tim told her about the DNA testing, she knew she had to move fast."

Caroline closed her eyes against the imagined horror of two innocent children drowning because of one woman's determination to secure an inheritance for her son.

They sat in silence for a long time and as she stayed curled in the loving warmth of Wes's arms, the world's ugliness seemed far, far away.

She smiled when he whispered, "Let's go look at our children." Then he added with a smile. "Cassie's always wanted to have a cookie party in bed. What do you think?"

"I'd like to come," she said as she gave him a soft kiss.

She was surprised to find herself laughing as they carried the cookie jar and a carton of soda pop into the bedroom. The two six-year-olds were curled up and asleep and looked like cherubs.

Wes stood there for a long moment, looking

down at his precious twins. His voice was husky as he reached out and touched them.

"Wake up, sleepyheads. It's celebration time!"

Epilogue

The Wainwright family home was a few miles out of Houston and had been built in the tradition of a Southern mansion with white columns and porticos. Wes's grandmother had been a Southern lady before her marriage and she'd brought that refined lifestyle to the Texas broad prairies when she married his grandfather.

"Of course, you'll probably want to make some changes to suit your own taste and style after we're married," Wes had assured her when he showed her through the mansion. "My parents left it pretty much the same while my brother and I were growing up."

"It's lovely," Caroline assured him. "There's

a wonderful sense of color and style." She couldn't believe that in a few days she'd be the lady of the house and not a wide-eyed visitor.

"Pamela was never comfortable here and spent most of her time in our Houston townhouse," he told her. "The ranch is about fifteen miles from here and the house there is roomy but not very fancy. That's where Stella and Shane chose to live." He sobered. "I've bought Shane some nearby acreage where he can develop his own ranch if that's what he decides to do and I'll provide some seasoned help for him. If he decides to go on to college, I'll take care of the finances." His voice broke. "I don't know why Stella didn't trust me to treat him fairly."

"Jealousy can twist everything," Caroline said softly, seeing the pain in his eyes. The past few weeks had been rough on him with the FBI investigation, Stella's indictment and closing up the lodge. The one bright spot was the DNA tests report which proved what they already knew but gave them some much-needed closure.

Caroline wrestled with the knowledge that Thomas had lied to her about Danny being the baby of a young, unmarried woman. Maybe that was the story Goodman gave him and Thomas pretended to know the girl personally in order to set Caroline's mind at ease. She was positive he didn't know the truth. Grateful for the miracle that had brought Danny to her, she knew Thomas would be glad for her newly found happiness.

A FEW DAYS LATER Caroline smiled at her reflection in a free-standing floor mirror in a luxurious bedroom. She wore a pink silk dress, cut low at the neck with delicate lace-edged sleeves. A long, slightly flared skirt fell to matching satin, high-heeled shoes. Wes's engagement present of diamond drop earrings swung saucily at her cheeks and a beautifully designed diamond ring sparkled on her finger.

"Don't you look absolutely perfect," Betty McClure exclaimed as she came into the guest bedroom. She and Jim had flown in from Denver the day before so Betty could be Caroline's matron of honor. Her light-blue gown with its straight lines and sheer overskirt was perfect for her.

"And so do you!" Caroline said drawing her over so they stood side by side in front of the mirror.

"I hope there are a dozen photographers snapping pictures," Betty said, grinning.

"Only one," Caroline said, smiling. "But we'll probably make the newspaper. I have no idea how many illustrious guests are coming to my wedding, but you're here and that's all that matters. Thank you for being my family," she said, hugging her.

"Uh-oh," Betty said as the strains of organ music floated up from the formal parlor down-stairs. "I hope Cassie and Danny stayed put the way I told them. If they've run off, I'll skin 'em." Then Betty added, "Shane was there waiting for Wes. I think he's a little nervous about all of this."

"I'm so glad Wes asked him to be best man," Caroline said. "He needs some strong family support right now."

"You'll win him over," Betty assured her as she handed Caroline her rosebud bridal bouquet. "Time to go. That handsome man of yours is waiting." She kissed Caroline on the cheek. "Isn't it amazing how wonderfully things turn out sometimes?"

"Yes," Caroline agreed with misty eyes. Last night when she and Wes had walked and talked in the garden, the velvet softness of his deep voice had been like a caress. She knew that the promises they made when they stood in each other's arms were as binding as the ones they would now repeat for others to hear. When Wes and Caroline had told the children that they were twins, Cassie had clapped her hands and Danny had given them a broad grin. They were a family now.

As Caroline descended the curved staircase, her happiness overflowed when she saw Danny, the ring bearer, and Cassie, the flower girl, waiting there.

The Wainwright twins were grinning happily at each other as if they had known from the beginning exactly who they were!